TEN RULES
for Living with
my SiSTER

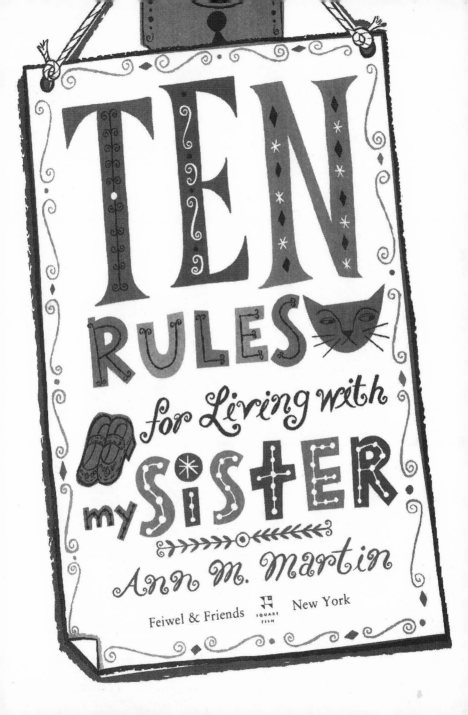

TEN RULES
for Living with my SISTER

Ann M. Martin

Feiwel & Friends · Square Fish · New York

SQUARE FISH

An Imprint of Macmillan

Square Fish and the Square Fish logo are trademarks of Macmillan and
are used by Feiwel and Friends under license from Macmillan.

Library of Congress Cataloging-in-Publication Data

Martin, Ann M.,
Ten rules for living with my sister / Ann M. Martin.
p. cm.
Summary: Nine-year-old Pearl and her popular, thirteen-year-old sister, Lexie,
do not get along very well, but when their grandfather moves in and the girls
have to share a room, they must find common ground.
ISBN: 978-1-250-01021-6
[1. Family life—New York (State)—New York—Fiction. 2. Sisters—Fiction.
3. Individuality—Fiction. 4. Grandfathers—Fiction. 5. Apartment houses—
Fiction. 6. New York (N.Y.)—Fiction.] I. Title.
PZ7.M3567585Ten 2011
[Fic]—dc22
2011009166

Originally published in the United States by Feiwel and Friends
First Square Fish Edition: September 2012
Square Fish logo designed by Filomena Tuosto
Book designed by Elizabeth Tardiff
mackids.com

5 7 9 10 8 6

AR: 4.7 / F&P: S / Lexile: 790 L

For my little sister
from her big sister

TEN RULES for Living with my SISTER

Half an hour ago my sister locked me out of her room. Then she opened her door long enough to hang this sign on it:

Then she closed the door again. It was the sixth time Lexie had hung the NO PEARL sign this month.

When I saw the sign, I went to my own room, put on

my pirate costume, and made a sign that said MY FEET SMELL. I hung it on Lexie's door underneath the NO PEARL sign and waited for my sister to come out.

I had to wait a long time, and I got a little bored. This was nothing new. I never know what to do with myself. Which is one of the differences between Lexie and me. Here are some others:

	☺ Lexie	☺ Pearl
Age	13 going on 14	9 (just barely)
Full Name	Alexandria	Pearl
Interests	violin ballay gymnastics soccer knitting school baby sitting	stuffed animals
Room	neat	sloppy
Friends ♡	Valerie (best friend) Sophia, Polly Chloe, Emma B. Emma F.	Justine (neighbor/ first-grader)
Boyfriend	Dallas	Bitey (cat) 🐱
Lipstick	yes	no

	☺ Lexie	☺ Pearl
Awards	yes	no
Chews Gum	no	yes
Pest	no	yes
Wears a Bra	yes	no
Has Had Apendix Out	no	yes
Has Thrown Up in a Taxicab	no	yes ☺
Has Own Key to Apartment	⚷ yes	no

First I waited for Lexie standing up. When my feet got tired, I sat down in the hallway. Bitey came along and crawled in my lap. Bitey's full name is Dr. Bitey McCrabby. He doesn't bite very often, and he's only crabby sometimes, which is why I let him be my boyfriend. I don't know where the doctor part of his name came from. A lot of things happened before I was born. One of them was naming Bitey. Lexie was three when she heard him meowing in the alley next to our apartment building. The vet figured Bitey was five months old then, which means he's ten now, which means I'm the youngest person in our family.

Lexie suddenly opened the door to her room and found Bitey and me sitting in the hall. The moment she saw us, she crossed her arms. "Pearl," she said, "do you know why I hung the sign? It's because if you are going to come in my room, I insist that you wear clothes. No more underwear visits. And I have to invite you first."

I shooed Bitey out of my lap, stood up, and removed my eye patch so I could see Lexie better. "How about if I wear my *new* underwear?" I asked. "It doesn't have any holes."

"No."

"What if *you're* in your underwear?"

"That will never happen."

My sister has a lot of rules these days, and many of them involve privacy.

Lexie turned around and noticed the MY FEET SMELL sign. She snorted, pulled it off of her door, walked down the hall, and stuck it on my door. Then she went back in her room and closed the door again. The NO PEARL sign was still hanging. I considered removing it, but the last time I did that, Lexie just made another one.

I threw away the MY FEET SMELL sign and changed out of my pirate costume and into a sweatshirt and a pair of jeans.

The doorbell rang, and I ran to answer it. No one

4

was in the hallway outside our apartment, which is #7F, which means it's the F apartment on the seventh floor.

"Justine!" I called. "I know you did that!"

Justine peeked out from where she'd been hiding behind the door to the service elevator. There are two elevators in our building, the regular one, which is in the hall, and the service elevator, which is behind a door marked SERVICE and is for delivery people and people who are walking their dogs. Almost everybody in our building who has a dog forgets to take the dogs up and down in the service elevator. No one cares about this except for Mrs. Mott, who lives on the tenth floor and is crabby and hates children in addition to dogs.

Justine was giggling. She jumped into the hall, letting the SERVICE door slam behind her. She plays this trick on me about 5x a week. It was funny the first 60x. Now it isn't so funny.

Justine Lebarro is seven years old and my best friend. She's in first grade at Emily Dickinson Elementary School, which is a few blocks away from our apartment building in the West Village, which is a neighborhood in New York City. Emily Dickinson was a poet. I'm in fourth grade at Emily Dickinson. (Lexie goes to a middle school, since she's thirteen-going-on-fourteen and is in eighth grade.)

One interesting thing is Justine is in first grade but

she's supposed to be in second, and I'm in fourth grade but I wish I were in third. Justine is on her second round of first grade since she hasn't exactly learned to read yet. All her last-year first-grade friends went on to second grade and she misses them. If I were Justine I would be thrilled. I would love to have gotten rid of Jill and Rachel and Katie and the rest of my last-year third-grade friends, but unfortunately we all went on to fourth grade together where, once again, I am the youngest kid in my class.

Justine lives down the hall in apartment #7D.

I held my finger to my lips. I had just had a great idea. "Shhh," I said to Justine. "Come on in."

"Why are you whispering?" she asked.

I shook my head and motioned for her to follow me.

We tiptoed past the kitchen and the family room and down the hall with the bedrooms and bathrooms and Mom's office. My bedroom is the smallest of all and it's at the very end of the hall. I closed my door quietly.

"Did you notice anything as we passed Lexie's room?" I asked Justine when we were sitting on my bed. Bitey had crawled into my lap, so Justine had moved to the exact opposite end of the bed since Bitey once almost bit her.

"No. I couldn't see in. Her door was closed."

"Exactly. Did you see what was on her door?"

"Oh. Is the NO PEARL sign up again?"

I nodded. "So I think we should scare Lexie."

Justine brightened. "Okay!"

"All right. You go back out in the hall and stand there and call, 'Lexie! Lexie!' I'll be right outside her door, and when she opens it to see what's wrong with you, I'll jump at her and go, 'Boo!' She hates that."

"Hates it," agreed Justine.

I opened my door and gave Justine a little push. She walked a few steps down the hall and said, "Lexie?"

I flattened myself against the wall by Lexie's door.

"Lexie?" said Justine again.

"Louder," I whispered.

"Lexie!!"

Lexie flung her door open. "What?"

"Boo!" I shouted.

Lexie jumped straight up in the air, as if her legs had cartoon springs attached to them. "Aughhh!" she shrieked.

Down the hall another door opened. My mother stuck her head out of her office. "Girls? What on earth is going on? Oh, hi, Justine."

"Hi, Mrs. Littlefield."

"Lexie? Pearl? What's the matter? I'm trying to work."

My mother, whose complete name is Adrienne Read Blackburn Littlefield, is a writer. She writes books for children. But all the books just say "By A. Littlefield." We are not supposed to disturb Mom unless it is an emergency.

Scaring Lexie was not an emergency. But that didn't

stop her from saying, "Pearl is being a giant pest. As usual."

"Do you think you can work this out yourselves, girls?"

Lexie glared at me. "Do not," she said, "I repeat, do *not* bother me again. Can't you see the sign?"

"I thought the NO PEARL sign meant I'm supposed to be dressed when I go in your room." Or was it that Lexie was supposed to invite me in? I wasn't sure. Sometimes Lexie's rules were confusing.

I looked at my mother, but she had already ducked back into her office. Before I was born, my bedroom was Mom's office, but then I came along and she had to move into a closet.

Lexie closed her door again, so Justine and I went back to my room and I found the game of Sorry! and got prepared to play the way I have to play when my opponent is Justine. In other words, I got prepared to remind her what every card means, and to help her figure out every move to make. I don't mind doing this. If I had trouble remembering rules, I would still want someone to play Sorry! nicely with me. We had barely started the game, though, when I realized that I hadn't done my chore for the day.

"Uh-oh," I said. "I forgot to get the mail. Want to come downstairs with me?"

Justine was on her feet in a flash. She likes to ride the

elevator without adults so that she can pretend she's nine years old and we're twins.

"Going to the lobby!" I called as I passed Lexie's room. "I have to get the mail." I grabbed the mailbox key and the spare key to #7F, which hang on a hook next to the bulletin board in the kitchen. Those are the only keys I ever get to use. Lexie has her own key to the apartment, Mom has a key to the apartment and six other keys, and Dad has a key to the apartment and five other keys. I have absolutely no keys of my own.

Justine and I rode the elevator to the lobby with Mrs. Mott, who was coming down from the tenth floor and who spoiled Justine's twin game by saying, "Justine Lebarro, where are your parents?"

Justine didn't answer her, and Mrs. Mott huffed away through the lobby and out onto Twelfth Street.

John was standing by the doorman's desk. "Hello, Pearl! Hello, Justine!" He's our favorite doorman. When Justine's balloon from the street fair slipped off her wrist and floated to the lobby ceiling, John got a ladder and rescued it.

"Hi, John," we said.

Just then Mr. Thompson, who is wrinkled and old and reminds me of my grandfather, Daddy Bo, came in from outside, walking his dog, Hammer, and got on the regular elevator, not the service one.

"It's a good thing Mrs. Mott didn't see that," I said to

John. Then I led Justine into the mailroom, found the box with 7F on it, opened it with the key, and took out three magazines and a handful of envelopes.

We rode the elevator back to the seventh floor and I looked through the mail while Justine said things like, "I am *so* excited about trying out for the fourth-grade play" and "Tomorrow let's go shopping for matching dresses, okay, twin?"

I let us back into my apartment with the spare key and returned both keys to the hook in the kitchen. I looked longingly at that hook and wished it were a key chain instead. One that was pink and had PEARL spelled out in blue and green gems from the crafts store. Then I sorted the mail into three piles: a pile of magazines for my parents, a little pile of envelopes for Dad, and another little pile of envelopes for Mom.

"Hey!" I exclaimed. "I got a postcard!"

Justine jumped up and down 3x. "Who's it from?" she asked.

"Daddy Bo." I looked at the postmark. New Jersey, so he wasn't on vacation or anything. "Here, I'll read it out loud. 'Dear Pearl, Hi! How are you? Yesterday Will Henderson and I went on a bus trip to Philadelphia.' Mr. Henderson is Daddy Bo's next-door neighbor," I told Justine. I turned back to the postcard. "'We saw the Liberty Bell and the Betsy Ross House.'"

"They went on a field trip?" asked Justine.

"A grown-up one, I guess. Anyway, then he writes, 'We didn't get home until ten at night! Love, Daddy Bo.'"

"Ten!" exclaimed Justine. "That's almost midnight."

I love Daddy Bo. He never asks how school is or who my friends are (besides Justine). And when he sees me, he never says how much I've grown. Three other things I like about Daddy Bo are:

1. He chews gum, the good kind, not sugarless
2. On my birthday he always gives me $5 in addition to a present
3. One time he went to Egypt and he rode a camel, which is a desert animal that has a hump and can spit

There was a knock on the door then, and Mrs. Lebarro called from the hallway, "Justine! Time to come home!"

At the same moment, my mother poked her head out of her office and called, "Pearl! Please start your homework."

Justine groaned and left. And I groaned and went to my room. I absolutely hate doing homework.

One good thing was that Lexie had taken down the NO PEARL sign.

2

Here's a fact about my father: He's punctual, which means he's always on time. Daddy Bo says you could set your clock by him. So when I heard the door to our apartment open I knew it must be 6:15, since that is the time Dad comes home from work. I looked at my clock. It said 6:14. I was about to call, "Dad, you're early!" but then the clock numbers changed to 6:15.

I had not finished my homework. In fact, I had not started it. I had looked out my window instead. That is how disgusting my homework was. I would rather have just stared out the window. My window faces into an airshaft. I have a view of bricks and pigeons.

What's too bad is that at the end of my second year of preschool, Lexie was starting to attract the attention of her teachers, who thought she was practically brilliant.

So Mom said, "Let's test Pearl!" like I was a new game at Toys "R" Us. They found someone to give me a test and it turns out I'm practically brilliant too, which is why my parents decided to start me in kindergarten then, which, if you ask me, was not a good idea. I think I could have used another year of preschool. For one thing, I would still be getting third-grade homework this year, and believe me, there is a LOT less homework in third grade than in fourth grade. For another thing, I would be the oldest in my class, not the youngest. And for a third thing, I would not have wound up in the same grade as Jill and Rachel and Katie.

I walked casually into the kitchen, trying to look like someone who had done all her homework.

"Hey, Dad," I said, all cool.

"Hi, pumpkin." My father is a university professor. He teaches economics, which is the serious study of money and taxes, etc., etc., etc.

"Did you finish your homework?" asked my mother.

"Well . . ."

"Did you *start* it?" asked Lexie from behind me.

I knew Lexie had been doing her own homework all afternoon and not even talking on the phone to her best friend, Valerie, or her new boyfriend, Dallas.

"Well . . . ," I said again.

My parents glanced at each other. "Pearl," said Mom, "do you remember our agreement?"

I did, since this was the first time my parents had had to make an agreement with me about homework. But I didn't want to admit it.

Luckily, just at this very moment, Bitey threw up in his water dish, so Dad hurried to clean it up and Lexie said, "Now *I'm* going to puke," and Mom said, "No, you're not. Go sit at the table." And my homework was forgotten.

The table my mother was referring to is in the big room that is the living room, family room, and dining room all rolled into one. While we eat dinner, we talk about our days. It's supposed to foster close family relationships.

My mother said, "I'm mad at one of my characters." This happens sometimes. She starts writing and then she gets stuck and blames it on a character. But I know she straightens things out, because her stories always get published.

"Which character?" I asked.

"Fiddle," Mom replied.

We had been hearing about Fiddle for quite some time. Fiddle was a horse with one blue eye and one red eye, which readers were supposed to find puzzling until they learned he was a stuffed animal horse and his eyes were buttons.

"Why are you mad at him?" Lexie wanted to know.

"I've written him into a corner," replied my mother.

"Then shouldn't you be mad at yourself?" I asked.

My mother smiled. "That's an excellent point, Pearl."

This was nice to hear since Lexie is usually the one who makes excellent points.

"Now that you've recognized that you're actually mad at yourself," Lexie said to Mom, "maybe you'll find a solution to your problem."

"Very astute," Mom replied.

Next my father said, "Well, the new school year is underway and I can safely say that this year's freshmen are more prepared for my introductory course than any of the freshmen before them."

I tried hard to appear interested, but the truth is that I don't really care about economics except for how much money is in my piggy bank, which is actually an elephant bank, which at that exact moment contained $8.91.

"That's a nice change, isn't it?" said Mom.

And Lexie said, "I wish we could take economics in middle school."

"Pearl? How was your day?" asked Dad.

I shrugged. "You know. Fine."

"Anything interesting happen?"

I thought for a moment. "No."

My parents looked at each other and sighed.

I sighed too. "I'm sorry," I said, "but I just went to school and came back. That was it."

I knew my parents wanted to hear me say that I had

gotten the highest score in my class on a math test, or that Jill and Rachel and Katie had invited me to do something with them. I couldn't even imagine what that something would be. Getting the highest math score was at least possible if I studied, but being invited somewhere by any one of my sworn enemies (let alone all three of them together) was about as likely as my suddenly needing a bra.

"I had an interesting day," Lexie spoke up. "Valerie decided to have a sleepover on Saturday night and she's inviting me and four other girls."

"Polly and the Emmas and who else?" I asked with interest.

"Gillian Meyer. You don't know her." Lexie turned back to Mom and Dad. "Valerie's parents are going to take us bowling."

"How nice," said Mom.

"And then also? After English class this morning?" said Lexie. "Dallas waited for me in the hall, so—"

"I thought Dallas was *in* your English class," I interrupted.

"He is."

"Then why did he have to wait in the hall? Why didn't he just talk to you in your classroom?"

"He wanted a little privacy," said Lexie.

"In the *hall*? You said the halls are always crowded."

"Pearl. Would you please let me finish speaking?"

Lexie turned back to our parents and rolled her eyes. "Anyway, Dallas is going to come over on Saturday. Is that okay? We're just going to watch a movie or some—"

"Lexie hung the NO PEARL sign this afternoon," I announced. "Again."

"Pearl! *Please!* Let me *fin*ish."

I looked first at Mom, then at Dad, with my saddest expression. "It was because of an underwear visit."

"Pearl!" cried my sister.

"She never put it up for an underwear visit before."

"Pearl came in wearing nothing but holey old underwear," exclaimed Lexie. "It was disgusting. I don't need that in my room."

"Girls," my father started to say.

"And anyway, I can put up the NO PEARL sign whenever I want, and for whatever reason." Lexie paused long enough to take a drink of water. "I was attempting to do my homework. 'Attempting' being the operative word," she added, which I have no idea what that meant except that it didn't sound good.

I stuck out my tongue at Lexie.

"Do you see this? Do you see this?" said Lexie, springing up from her chair and pointing at my tongue. "Look what I have to put up with!"

"Lexie, please sit down," said my father. Sometimes he says, "Lexie, resume yourself," but he knew Lexie wasn't in a mood for humor.

Lexie plunked herself back down in her seat. "Dad. Mom. Pearl is such a baby sometimes. She and Justine played a stupid trick on me this afternoon. And Pearl walks around wearing that pirate costume—"

"At least I was dressed," I said.

"And she interrupts me *all* the *time*! Like right now!"

I slumped in my chair and stopped listening to Lexie. There was no point. Instead, I made a little list in my head.

Five Reasons Lexie Thinks She's So Great

1. She almost gets straight A's.
2. She has a boyfriend and his name is Dallas, which is not a plain name like Bob or Jim.
3. She has a best friend who is her own age, plus more friends, including the two Emmas.
4. She is allowed to go places without a grown-up. Of course, she has to stay in our neighborhood, but she can still go to the movies and to stores and over to her friends' apartments, where they put on nail polish.
5. She has her own cell phone and her own computer and her own KEY TO THE APARTMENT.

It took a long time to think up that list but when I was finished, Lexie was *still* talking about her day. When you have a lot of friends and a lot of interests, you also have a lot to say.

Lexie was talking and talking and talking. What I heard was blah, blah, blah-dy, blah, blah.

I pretended to drop my napkin. I mean, I actually did drop it, but I dropped it on purpose, not by accident. When I leaned down to pick it up, I looked under the table and saw that Lexie had slipped off her shoes, the new purple ones she had bought the day before. She had said they were expensive but that she had been saving and saving her money until she had enough to pay for them without borrowing anything from Mom and Dad. (Good economics.) She added that they were *sheek*, which I don't know what that means, and that Valerie and Emma B. were each going to get a pair too. Lexie had worn her new shoes nonstop since she bought them, except for when she was in bed last night. And except for right now.

I straightened up in my chair and made a great show of refolding my napkin. Then I wiggled my right foot around under the table until I felt Lexie's shoes, and I slid them under my chair. I watched Lexie's face and Mom's face and Dad's face very carefully. I smiled as if I were really enjoying Lexie's story about how Dallas was so smart that he had to take a math test 2x, just to prove that he hadn't cheated the first time, when he got a 100% plus extra credit.

No one saw what I was doing. I pretended to drop my napkin again, and this time I shoved the shoes in back of the floor-length curtains behind me.

I waited.

It wasn't until dinner was finally over and we were clearing our places that Lexie suddenly leaned down and exclaimed, "They're gone!"

"What?" said Mom. "What are gone?"

"My new shoes!"

"They're gone off your feet?" I asked.

"No! I mean, yes. I mean, I was wearing them and I took them off during dinner, and now they aren't under the table."

My parents got down on their hands and knees and peered around with Lexie.

"The only thing down here is Bitey," said my father.

"Are you *sure* you were wearing them when dinner began?" asked my mother.

"Yes!"

"Maybe you took them off when Bitey barfed," I suggested. "To keep them clean. Maybe you should go look in your room."

Lexie shook her head. "That would be pointless."

"Well, go check your room anyway. They couldn't have just disappeared," said my father sensibly.

My lips formed themselves into a tiny smile. "No. That would be impossible," I said. "They couldn't have just disappeared."

Everyone looked at my small smile.

"Pearl? Do you know anything about this?" asked Mom, and I heard a tone in her voice. It was the You're-Walking-on-Thin-Ice tone, which, well, to be honest, sometimes I think it would be exciting to actually fall through the ice and see what's underneath.

My smile grew a teensy bit larger.

"What did you do with my shoes?" Lexie demanded. She thumped her fist on the table, which made the silverware jump, but my parents did not say one word about this.

"Pearl?" said my father, and now *his* voice had a tone, only this one was the I've-Almost-Reached-the-End-of-My-Rope tone, and so since I knew what would happen if he did reach the end of his rope and I didn't want my art supplies confiscated again, I paid attention when he continued by saying, "Please give Lexie's shoes back to her."

I pulled the curtains aside. There were the shoes. Lexie pounced on them and jammed them back on her feet. She glared at me. "I am no longer speaking to you," she announced.

Then she stomped off down the hall and slammed the door to her room.

P.S. Confiscated = Taken Away

3

I am no stranger to the silent treatment. When Lexie is mad at me she shouts, "I'm not speaking to you!" Sometimes after that she whips her head away from me, or turns her back, or stomps into her room and slams the door.

And then sometimes one of my parents will mutter, "Teenagers." (They only mean Lexie, not me, since you don't qualify as a teenager until you are thirteen.)

"Will I be like that when I'm Lexie's age?" I asked Dad once.

"Probably," he had replied sadly. "But luckily it will just be a phase."

I decided to sit outside Lexie's room again, under the NO PEARL sign, which she had re-hung five seconds after announcing that she wasn't speaking to me.

"Pearl," said my mother, "I think you're asking for trouble. Come away from Lexie's door, please. Why don't you show me your homework so I can make sure you completed all your assignments."

Uh-oh. My homework. "I have a little to finish up," I told her. And I rushed into my room, did three worksheets in record time, and then waved them back and forth in front of Mom's face while she was on the telephone. After that I put on my pajamas and stepped into the hallway. Lexie was just coming out of the bathroom.

"Hey," I said, all cool again.

She didn't answer.

"So how long do you think your silent treatment is going to last this time?"

Still no answer.

"Couldn't you just give me a clue?"

No answer.

"If you tell me then I won't have to keep bugging you."

No answer. Lexie closed the door to her room.

I stood in the hall and called, "Lexie! Oh, Lexie! How long is the silent treatment going to last?" I counted to five. "Lexie! Oh, Lexie! I *said*, how long is the silent treatment going to last?" I waited five more seconds. "Lexie! Oh, Lexie! How long is—"

Lexie flung her door open so fast that the NO PEARL sign almost blew off. "I DON'T KNOW! UNTIL I'M NOT MAD ANYMORE, OKAY?" she yelled.

"Boy, you sure aren't very good at the silent treatment," I told her, and she slammed the door.

The next morning at breakfast, I said, "Lexie, is the silent treatment over yet?"

And Lexie said, "Mom, I need a new library card."

So the silent treatment was definitely not over.

After breakfast, Justine and I rode the elevator down to the lobby with Dad and Lexie.

"Hi, Lexie," said Justine in a friendly manner.

"Hey." Lexie sounded grumpy so she was probably still mad about being boo-ed by us the day before.

In the lobby, Lexie said, "Dad, Dallas is going to meet me here and walk me to school."

"Okay," replied Dad, and he kissed the top of her head. "Have a good day."

"Bye, Lexie!" I called as John held the door open.

Lexie just stood there in her purple shoes, staring at a wall.

"Silent treatment," I whispered to John, and pointed to Lexie with my thumb.

"It won't last," John whispered back.

"I know."

Dad and Justine and I turned right and began the walk to Emily Dickinson Elementary. Dad walked in the middle and Justine and I held his hands. We passed Quik-Mart, which is a delicatessen, and Universal, which is a dry cleaner, and The Bagel Place, which you can figure out, and New World, which is a coffee shop, and Steve-Dan's, which sells art supplies, and Happy-Go-Lucky, which is something of a mystery. Also, we passed Alice, who is a woman who sits out on her stoop with her little white dog and spends all morning saying, "Snowball, don't bite. Snowball, come back here. Snowball, don't eat that. Oh, Snowball, how did you get to be so naughty?" You would think she would be annoyed by Snowball's behavior, but she always smiles at him quite fondly, just like mothers and fathers smile at their children and think they're cute even when they're clearly not.

When we reached school, we said good-bye to my father, and Justine ran to room 1B, which is a first-grade class, which is right by the front door. I ambled along the hall to room 4C. My teacher's name is Mr. Potter. Sometimes this one boy in my class calls him Mr. Potty behind his back, but most of us like him. He's okay as teachers go.

"Hi, Pearl," he said as I slid into my seat. I sit directly in front of Mr. Potter's desk. This is not so he can keep an eye on me, but because no one else wanted to sit that close to the teacher. Also, the other kids wanted to sit near their friends, so on the first day of school there was a great scrambling around in order for Jill and Rachel and Katie to flock together in the back row, and Evan and Ryan to sit together by the windows, and Kenny and Greg to sit directly behind Evan and Ryan, and Katrina and Tracy to sit anywhere as long as they're together, and blah, blah, blah-dy, blah, blah. Only four of the strays—Leslie, James Brubaker the Third, Elyse, and I—wound up in the first row. And I wound up right under Mr. Potter's nose. The front of my desk touches the back of his desk. When we're both sitting there, I look straight into his eyes, which is embarrassing, and not at all like staring into Bitey's eyes, which if you do it long enough he'll turn away and lick his paw.

If the Three Bad Things hadn't happened last year I might have scrambled around on the first day of school in order to sit next to someone special too. Jill maybe. But they had happened, and everyone remembered them, even kids who were in the *other* third-grade classes, which is why I wished I could be in third grade *now* with kids who had never heard of the Three Bad Things.

"Hi," I answered Mr. Potter. And this was when I remembered that the three worksheets I had done the night before were at home on my bed. Or maybe under it. But definitely not in my backpack.

"Pearl, how would you like to collect everyone's homework today?" asked Mr. Potter.

I would not like to do that at all, but I knew that the only possible answer to this question was, "Okay. Thank you." So I said, "Okay. Thank you," and stood up.

Being the homework collector was slightly good but

mostly bad. It was good, at least for me, because if I was the one collecting the homework then Mr. Potter might not notice if I didn't hand in my own assignments. But it was bad because no one likes the homework collector. Everyone, Mr. Potter included, could watch and see if someone (apart from the actual collector) didn't hand over his worksheets, and then Mr. Potter would write that person's name on the upper left hand corner of the blackboard. In my case, being the homework collector was especially bad, though, because as I walked up and down the aisles everyone watched me and remembered the Three Bad Things and silently called me various names.

If you must know, the Three Bad Things happened at the beginning, the middle, and the end of third grade. Each thing was worse than the one before, so that the last one, which took place on our end-of-the-year class trip to the Museum of Natural History, was the worst of all—and the one everyone remembers the best. Also, when you find out what the Three Bad Things are you can sort of see how I wound up with my reputation as a baby.

The first bad thing happened on Day #1 of third grade when I showed up with my Mickey Mouse ears, the ones with my name written in fancy script like *Pearl* across the front. We had been to Disney World over the summer and I couldn't wait to show off the hat. As it turned out, that wasn't such a good idea. The problem wasn't the hat, which the other kids liked okay. The problem was that I planned to present it during Show and Tell. When we reached the end of the day and Mrs. Van Horn, our teacher, hadn't said anything about Show and Tell, I raised my hand and I was like, "Excuse me, Mrs. Van Horn, we only have six minutes until the bell. Are we going to have enough time?"

"Enough time for what, Pearl?"

"For Show and Tell." I almost added, "Duh."

Mrs. Van Horn looked surprised, but no one said anything until finally Katie exploded with laughter and exclaimed, "We don't have Show and Tell in third grade!"

Well, I didn't know that. (How come everyone else did?)

Soon the whole class was laughing except Mrs. Van Horn, because teachers aren't allowed to laugh at their students, including when they want to.

Eventually the laughing died down, but the memory stuck and everyone talked about Show and Tell until December 3rd, which was the day I wet my pants while I was giving a book report. This incident was entirely Mrs. Van Horn's fault, since I had already asked her 2x that morning if I could go to the girls' room and she had asked me back if I couldn't please wait and go at lunchtime. Then when I wet my pants, she said in front of the whole class, "Oh, I'm sorry, Pearl. I should have let you tinkle when you asked."

So then for the next six months everyone including the kids in the other third-grade classes talked about my tinkle. And they hadn't forgotten about it by the day of our trip to the museum. In fact, I heard both Show and Tell and tinkle mentioned on our bus ride uptown. (I was sitting by myself in a two-person seat and pretending that I liked having all that space to spread out in.)

The trip went okay until the very end when I was standing in front of a dinosaur and all of a sudden I realized that no one else in my class was with me. I looked around the room, which was the size of an airport, and it was just me and the dinosaur. So then I ran into another room and there were a lot of people in it, but no one from my class. I ran into another room and another and another, but all I saw were groups of kids from the wrong schools, and adults who were strangers.

Finally I shouted, "Help, police!" and in a few minutes an officer was at my side asking what was wrong, and I said that Jill's mother, who was named Mrs. DiNunzio and who was one of the class parents on our trip, was supposed to be keeping an eye on me and that obviously she hadn't done her job. It took a lot of sorting out, but eventually the officer found my class and Mrs. Van Horn and Mrs. DiNunzio and the other parent helpers. I think all the adults got in a little trouble, especially Jill's mother, and on the way home not only did I have a whole seat to myself on the bus again, but a couple of rows in front and back of me were empty too, even though it meant that some of the kids had to sit three to a seat.

So, Three Bad Things. Show and Tell, tinkle, and Help, police. I know that's what my fourth-grade classmates think about whenever they see me.

I walked around our room now, going up and down the aisles in an orderly fashion, from the wall side of the room to the windows side of the room. At each desk, I held out my hand and waited for three papers to be placed in it. I always checked them, and it was a good thing because William had only done one worksheet, but he tried to trick me by slipping two sheets of notebook paper underneath it. I caught him right away, and handed back the blank pages.

"Tinkle," he whispered, which caused quite a bit of giggling even though Mr. Potter was already writing *William* in the corner of the board.

In the back row, Jill handed me her three perfect papers with a smirk. She didn't mention Help, police, but she did say, "I saw you walking to school this morning." And I knew what she meant was that she had seen me *and Justine* walking to school *holding hands* with my father. Everyone in fourth grade walks to school with a grown-up or an older brother or sister. But no one else in fourth grade has a first-grade best friend. (For some reason, no one cares that Justine is nearly eight.) Plus, maybe it was time to stop holding my father's hand.

Or not.

"How did that blue stuff get on your head?" I asked, and Jill went, "What? What?" and in seconds, Rachel and Katie were pawing through her hair like monkeys, looking for absolutely nothing.

When I got to the last desk, I collected Evan's worksheets while he sang a little made-up song about Show and Tell, and I handed the stack to Mr. Potter.

Our first subject of the day was math, so I sat and thought about my pirate costume and how a hook hand would really spruce it up, but I didn't have enough money for a hook hand and Mom and Dad didn't seem inclined to buy me one. Maybe they would change their minds at Halloween.

I knew that the rest of the fourth-grade girls would think pirate costumes were babyish—except maybe at Halloween—but I didn't care. I am an original.

"Pearl?" said Mr. Potter.

"What? I mean, yes?"

"Do you know how Katie arrived at that answer?"

"What answer?" I said.

Mr. Potter sighed.

I heard giggling from the back row. I turned around and glared at Jill. Then I pointed to my head and frowned as if to say, "What is going on with that blue stuff in your hair?" Jill's eyes widened and she began pulling her hair down in front of her eyes and squinting at it.

I felt satisfied.

I felt so satisfied that I wrote a note to Justine that said,

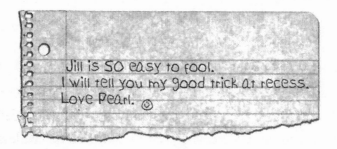

Jill is SO easy to fool.
I will tell you my good trick at recess.
Love Pearl. ☺

I planned to pass the note to Justine if I saw her in the corridor, but then I remembered that Justine can't read yet except for maybe *dog* and *cat*, so I crumpled up the note and stuck it far back in my desk.

At Emily Dickinson, we don't have a playground, so recess is held on the roof of our school. There's a fence all around the edge to keep you from falling off, which if you fell it would be three stories. And the roof has been covered with some kind of rubber. There are basketball hoops up there (with giant nets behind them to keep the balls from flying over the fence and clomping people on the street below), and places where you can play hop-scotch and four-square, but there aren't any swings or climbing bars so it isn't exactly a true playground.

At recess Jill and Rachel and Katie and some of the other girls in my class usually huddle together and write notes to boys, which I don't think they ever send. There's a "no electronics" rule at Emily Dickinson, but apparently there isn't a "no makeup" rule because Jill brings a little bag of nail polish bottles to recess, and the girls paint flowers on their fingernails after they've finished writing the notes. A couple of times I have hovered around, sort of wanting to join in, but the word "tinkle" crops up pretty quickly. Anyway, I couldn't care less about painting flowers on my nails.

I play with Justine instead.

The first-grade girls think Justine is weird, since she's nearly two years older than some of them. On the other hand, she has a fourth-grade best friend, which they think is cool. So does Justine. And if I do say so myself, I'm a pretty good friend for her to have, since I never make remarks about her school problems, and I don't mind helping her with Sorry!, etc., etc., etc.

The fourth-grade girls sometimes look up from their note-writing and nail-painting and say things like,

"Kindergarten baby," which makes no sense since Justine isn't in kindergarten and neither am I. Also, "kindergarten baby" isn't very original.

Just before recess was over, Jill said to me, "What's the matter? Won't anyone your own age play with you?"

And I said, "Why, thank you, Jill. I'd *love* to paint my nails." I reached for her polish.

Jill scowled and snatched the polish back, and then I pointed to her hair.

"Ha! I'd have to be pretty stupid to fall for *that* again," said Jill.

And I said, "Okay, don't believe me," and stared really hard at her forehead. "I just hope your mother can get it out before it's too late," I added.

Once again, Jill made Katie and Rachel search through her hair, and I watched them and tried not to laugh.

By the time school was over, my name had been added to the corner of the blackboard. Mr. Potter had sorted through our homework papers during recess.

"Did you lose yours or forget them?" he asked me.

"Forgot them," I replied, which was true, although I also wasn't sure where they were. But I did not believe that they were officially lost.

When the bell rang I picked up Justine at the door of room 1B and we waited in front of school with a monitor until Lexie came to walk us home. Here is what Lexie said when she saw us: zero.

The silent treatment was in full swing.

"Wow, this must be some kind of record," I said as we passed The Bagel Place.

Lexie studied the sign in their window even though the same sign had been hanging there for the past eight months.

"I know you aren't talking to Pearl, but are you talking to *me*?" Justine asked Lexie.

"I guess," Lexie answered.

"Tell Lexie that I want to know when the silent treatment is going to end," I said to Justine.

"Lexie, Pearl wants to know when the silent treatment is going to end."

"Too bad for her," Lexie replied, and kept on walking.

4

Lexie wanted to walk ten steps ahead of Justine and me, that's how annoyed she was. But the rule is that she has to walk *with* us when she brings us home from school. So she was stuck. She clunked up Sixth Avenue in her purple shoes, lugging her violin. She did not look at us or speak to us.

"She's really mad this time," Justine whispered to me.

I agreed with her, but Lexie had been really mad plenty of other times, so it didn't mean much.

We turned onto Twelfth Street and marched along to our apartment building, all of us carefully avoiding Mrs. Mott, who was trying to hail a cab and didn't see us anyway.

"Hi, John," I said as we entered the lobby.

"Hi, John," Justine said.

Lexie gave John a stiff-fingered wave.

"Hello, girls," he replied. Then he said, "Why did the golfer wear two pairs of pants?"

"I don't know. Why?" I asked.

"In case he got a hole in one!"

I liked the joke, even though I know almost zero about golf. Lexie allowed herself a teensy smile. But Justine said, "I don't get it." Justine mostly likes jokes about why things cross the road.

"I'll explain it to her later," I whispered to John.

Lexie's teensy smile had given me an idea. While we were riding the elevator up to the seventh floor I said, "Hey, Lexie, what's black and white and black and white and black and white?" My sister stared at the elevator buttons, so I answered myself, "A skunk rolling down a hill!"

Justine burst into loud laughter, but Lexie's face was all still, like one of those British guards, the ones who wear the tall furry hats and aren't allowed to talk or laugh or even smile.

Justine got excited. "I know one! I know one!" she cried. "Lexie, why did the farmer cross the road?"

The elevator squeaked to a stop and Lexie hurried off of it.

"To get the runaway chicken!" Justine called after her.

"You have to tell the regular chicken joke first," I

reminded Justine. "Otherwise the second part doesn't make sense."

"Oh," said Justine.

Lexie was already at the end of the hall, using her personal key to unlock our door.

Justine knocked on #7D and when her mother let her in she said, "Mom, I'm going to play at Pearl's, okay?"

"Okay," said her mother.

"Don't worry," I told Mrs. Lebarro. "I'll give her a snack."

"Do you have animal crackers?" Justine asked me as we walked to #7F.

Even for Justine this seemed a little babyish, but I didn't say anything except, "I doubt it." I knocked on my own door, since it had locked automatically behind Lexie. Lexie opened it wordlessly and retreated to her room. This was definitely a silent treatment record.

After I told my mother that I was home, and after Justine and I had eaten a non-animal-cracker snack, I said, "Justine, we have to find a way to make Lexie talk. Or at least smile."

"She talked to me," Justine pointed out. We were sitting on my bed again.

"Sort of. But she's still mad, and besides, I want her to talk to *me*."

"What should we do?"

"I'm not sure. Our jokes didn't work."

"Maybe they weren't funny enough."

I rested my chin on my hand. "See if you think this one is funny," I said after a few moments. "How many elephants can fit in a taxi? . . . Three in the front and three in the back!"

Justine hesitated before laughing uncertainly. At last she said, "Then where does the taxi driver sit?"

I sighed. "I guess it isn't funny."

Bitey poked his nose into my room.

"I know what would be funny!" exclaimed Justine. "Let's dress up Bitey like he's in a beauty pageant. I mean, *you* should dress him up," she added, edging away from him as he approached her, his tail switching.

"A beauty pageant," I repeated thoughtfully. "Hmm. I guess I could put my Lady Pamela doll's clothes on him. She even has a crown."

"Yes!" cried Justine, as she slid farther away from Bitey.

It wasn't easy wrenching the crown off Lady Pamela (who I hadn't played with in years), but I managed at last, and then I took off her satiny gown, only ripping it a little in the back. I was pretty sure my mother wouldn't notice. I hauled Bitey into my lap and tugged the dress on him so quickly that it was a full five seconds before he suddenly began flailing around and howling. (Justine escaped into the hall.) I held tight to Bitey and slipped the crown on his head, hooking it over his ears. Bitey shook his head and the crown flew off and landed in my wastebasket. I tried a second time, and was prepared when Bitey shook his head again. I clutched the crown tightly and grabbed Bitey in the dress and whisked him into the hallway where Justine and I stood outside Lexie's door.

"Now what?" I whispered. "How are we going to get Lexie to come out?" I'd been thinking that maybe I could knock on her door and say something tantalizing like, "And now . . . here to entertain you . . . please welcome our next contestant . . . the charming . . . the talented . . . Dr. Bitey McCrabby!"

But before I could say a word, Justine scrunched up her face and screamed, "Help! Fire! Fire!"

All at the same moment, my mother's door flew open, Lexie's door flew open, and Bitey, a blur of fur and claws, emitted an angry *MROWL!* followed by a hiss, and flew past my mother and into the family room where he jumped up on a table and knocked over a lamp. The crown had flown off again, but he was still wearing the dress.

"Uh-oh," I said.

"Uh-oh," Justine said.

"Girls!" cried my mother. "Get out of the apartment right now!" And she ran into the kitchen and found the fire extinguisher.

It was quite a while before everything was straightened out and I had apologized to my mother and Lexie, undressed Bitey, found the crown, and put Band-Aids on the worst of my scratches.

Justine got sent home, and then my mother stood in the family room and glared first at me and then at the lamp, which luckily was not broken. I set the lamp back on the table.

"I wasn't the one who shouted 'Fire,'" I pointed out. "That was Justine. And I didn't know she was going to do it."

My mother was having a cup of tea to calm her nerves. "I think we all need a little quiet time," she said. "Why don't you go start your homework?"

"Okay," I replied, even though I knew I could finish my homework in about half an hour and planned to do it after dinner.

My mother disappeared into her office again, and I passed Lexie's door (closed, as usual, with scritchy violin noises coming from the other side of it), went to my room, and took off my jeans and my Cowgirl Hall of Fame T-shirt. I was hot after all the excitement.

I sat at my desk in my underwear and thought for a while. I really, really, *really* wanted the silent treatment to end. I knew I had annoyed Lexie by hiding her shoes, and also by booing her and interrupting her story. But Lexie had annoyed me by calling me a baby. Still, if Lexie wouldn't speak to me, how could I tell her my jokes? How could I ask her questions about her new boyfriend, or ask her for favors? (I was hoping one day to be able to make a prank call to Jill using Lexie's cell phone.)

There was only one thing to do, and that was apologize—if Lexie would listen to me.

I was still very hot, but I remembered what Lexie had said about underwear visits, so I put on my frog slippers before I knocked on her door.

After a moment I heard my sister call, "Who is it?"

I wished I could say, "It's Mom," and sound convincing, but I knew I couldn't. "It's me, your sister, Pearl," I replied. I waited a moment before adding, "I want to apologize. I'm really sorry I hid your shoes. I know I shouldn't have done that. And I want to apologize for when Justine and I scared you. And for interrupting you at dinner last night. I already apologized for today, so I guess I don't have to do that again. . . . Lexie? I'm very, very, very, very, very, very sorry."

At last Lexie's door opened a crack. All I could see was one side of her lips and one nostril and a little part of an eye. "Do you mean it?" she asked.

"I truly and honestly mean it."

"Okay." She opened her door all the way and saw me standing there in my slippers and underwear. "Pearl!" she exclaimed. "I can't believe this! I said no more underwear visits! That's why I put up the NO PEARL sign in the first place."

"It's not an underwear visit. I'm wearing slippers too."

Lexie shook her head. "You are—," she started to say, but I guess she couldn't think of what word to fill in because then she just shook her head and closed the door.

The NO PEARL sign was still up, and the silent treatment was back in place.

I sat at my desk again. Maybe I should do my homework after all. I looked at my science book for ten seconds, and then I decided to write a postcard to Daddy Bo instead. It said:

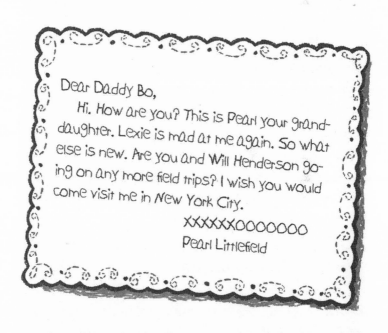

Dear Daddy Bo,

Hi. How are you? This is Pearl your granddaughter. Lexie is mad at me again. So what else is new. Are you and Will Henderson going on any more field trips? I wish you would come visit me in New York City.

XXXXXXOOOOOOO
Pearl Littlefield

I found a stamp for the postcard and then I went on a search for the missing worksheets and finally found them under a pile of clothes on the floor. I could hand them in tomorrow.

At 6:16, Dad came home.

"You're late!" I shouted from my room.

I walked down the hall. I wasn't going to look at Lexie's door since I had decided I was officially mad back at her, but I couldn't help noticing out of the corner of my eye that the NO PEARL sign was gone. I was about to knock on the door and thank my sister when I saw that another sign was hanging in its place. This is what it looked like:

Since Lexie is not a very good artist it took me a while to realize that the new sign meant NO UNDERWEAR VISITS.

I considered the sign during dinner. It seemed to me that you shouldn't have to think too much about a sign to figure out what it means. A sign should be very plain, like a stop sign or the NO PEARL sign. I remembered one time when my family and I had gone to a restaurant for dinner and I'd walked into the men's room because the sign on the door hadn't said MEN. Instead it had shown a picture of a bull wearing a cowboy hat. The sign on the door across from it had shown a picture of a cow wearing a bonnet. Those were not good signs because animals don't normally wear clothes. And when they do, like when I dress up Bitey, they can put on anything. They aren't choosy.

At any rate, Lexie's NO UNDERWEAR VISITS sign wasn't as bad as the bull and cow signs, but it wasn't very good either. I thought I could do a better job, so after dinner I got out my markers and made a new sign. It looked like this:

I knew there was no point in knocking on Lexie's door again. She wouldn't open it for me. Instead I waited until she came out to use the bathroom. The moment she was fully in the hallway I thrust the sign at her.

"Here," I said. "I made this for your door. It's, well, slightly better than your sign. Just *slightly*." I tried to sound modest.

Lexie stared at the sign. Then she snatched it from me and went back in her room without taking her shower. I don't know what she did with the new sign, but she didn't take down the one she had made. She just left it hanging there. It might as well have said Show and Tell, tinkle, Help, police.

On Saturday, Lexie's new boyfriend came over. They had talked on the phone 6x the night before, and Lexie had left her door open so I would be sure to hear the conversations. My sister was all, "Hee-hee-hee, Dallas. That is *so* funny!" and, "Oh, Dallas, *then* what did you say?" which doesn't really sound like Lexie. But I guess that's what a new boyfriend will do to you.

When our doorbell rang on Saturday morning I called, "I'll get it!"

"No, you won't!" Lexie ran ahead of me down the hall and reached the door first.

"Mom!" I wailed.

My parents were sitting together in the family room. Parts of the newspaper were everywhere. That is what Mom and Dad do on Saturday and Sunday mornings.

They read the newspaper. And drink coffee. They always get a little excited about it, like the newspaper and coffee are actually comics and bubble gum.

"Pearl, let Lexie answer the door. It's her friend," said Mom. She and Dad stood and began gathering up the newspaper pages.

"It's not her friend, it's her *boy*friend," I replied.

"Nevertheless," said Dad, and he and Mom carried their papers and coffee mugs into the kitchen and settled themselves into the two small, uncomfortable chairs by the window.

I peeked into the hallway and watched Dallas follow my sister into the family room. They sat next to each other on the couch. They sat so close that their arms were mushed up against each other.

I went to my room for a while. I looked out the window. It was raining.

I stood up and walked back to the family room. I leaned against the doorway with my hand on my hip. Lexie and Dallas were watching a DVD. I didn't say anything, so Lexie reached for the remote and paused the movie. "May I help you?" she asked.

I examined Dallas. I wanted to know why Lexie had said he was hot when she was talking to Valerie the day before. He didn't look like much of anything to me except maybe a poodle. That's how curly his hair was.

"I just wanted to meet Dallas," I replied. I knew my parents had met him once before, which was why they were giving Lexie and Dallas their privacy now. If they hadn't met him, the five of us would have been sitting in the family room together.

"Pearl, Dallas. Dallas, Pearl," said Lexie, and unpaused the movie.

I waved at Dallas anyway and he waved back. I thought he had kind eyes. My big sister had chosen a nice boyfriend.

I said to Dallas over the movie sounds, "My sister isn't talking to me."

"What? What on earth do you mean?" Lexie was suddenly at attention. She paused the movie again. Then she stood up and put her arm across my shoulder. "Pearl's very young," she said to Dallas. "She exaggerates." Then, seeing the disgusted look on my face, she added, "She has a wonderful imagination, though. Everyone says so."

Dallas smiled at me.

"By the way," Lexie continued, "I really like your outfit, Pearl."

Translation: I'm glad you're not in your underwear and frog slippers, Pearl.

I went into the kitchen. Mom and Dad were still reading and drinking coffee. The rain was still falling.

"Can I invite Justine over?" I asked.

"No, but you may go to her apartment," said Dad.

Well, that was no good. I wanted Justine to meet Dallas. She had a lot of questions about boyfriends.

I carried Bitey into my bedroom. "Bitey," I said, "you are my boyfriend, so I should probably kiss you." I looked at his little spotted cat lips and made a decision. "I'll just kiss you on the top of your head." I leaned over to kiss Bitey's head and he swatted my face.

I wondered if Lexie and Dallas had ever kissed.

I went back to the family room. The movie was still playing.

This time when I stood in the doorway Lexie said, "*Hi*, Pearl! What's up?"

"I was just wondering if—"

From behind me Mom said, "Hello, Dallas. It's good to see you again. Would you like a soda or anything?"

"No, thank you, Mrs. Littlefield," replied Dallas politely.

My big sister had chosen a nice and polite boyfriend.

I trailed into the kitchen after my mother. I crouched down on the floor and looked to see if anything interesting was under the stove. I used a coat hanger to slide out three of Bitey's dusty plastic balls, the ones with bells inside.

My boyfriend chased plastic balls.

"Pearl?" said my father. "Don't you know what to do with yourself?"

"I want to invite Justine over."

"I already said that you may go over there, but that she may not come over here."

I heaved an enormous sigh and went back to my bedroom.

I sat around some more and then I picked up Bitey and carried him, flailing and meowing, to the family room.

Dallas smiled when he saw us. "Well, who's this?" he asked.

Lexie paused the movie again and said sweetly, "Pearl just *adores* our cat, Bitey, don't you, Pearl?"

"I named him," I announced.

Lexie smiled indulgently at me and said quietly to Dallas, "She wasn't even born when we got Bitey." Then she raised her voice to its normal level. "It's fun to pretend things, isn't it, Pearl?"

I narrowed my eyes at my sister. I was absolutely 100% positive that the silent treatment wasn't over and that Lexie was just putting on a show for her boyfriend. I was also absolutely 100% positive that Lexie wanted to get back to the movie, but that she didn't want to say anything mean to me in front of Dallas.

I set Bitey on the floor and returned to my room.

Maybe, I thought, I could help Dallas get to know Lexie better. I felt that he needed to know the real Lexie, not the sweety/fakey one who was sitting next to him in the family room. This was when I remembered where Mom and Dad had put some of Lexie's and my baby things. I rummaged around in the linen closet in the hall until I found the box labeled LEXIE. I had looked through it many, many times (it was more interesting than the much smaller box labeled PEARL), and I knew just what to show Dallas.

A few minutes later I was standing in the family room once more.

"How nice. Pearl's back," said my sister, and she paused the movie.

Dallas looked at me pleasantly, and I held a plastic bag toward him. "Did you ever see this?" I asked.

I think that right at that moment Lexie realized what was in the bag, but she was too late to do anything about it. I had already opened the bag and was pulling out a grimy piece of blue fabric.

"This is Lexie's baby blanket," I said. "His name is Snuffy."

"Pearl!" shrieked my sister, leaping to her feet.

"Snuffy's kind of disgusting, isn't he?" I asked Dallas.

Snuffy was actually revolting. He looked like he'd never been washed, and he had a crusty yellow stain on one corner. I held him up by two of the clean corners and turned him around so Dallas could inspect both sides.

"Over here," I continued, as if I were taking Dallas on a tour, "is a thin patch where Lexie used to rub him with her thumb while she was asleep. And this hole is from when she got him caught in the elevator doors. Mom said she yelled so loudly that the doormen could hear her at the bottom of the elevator shaft. And"—I leaned in close to inspect something on the binding—"I don't know what this brown stuff is."

Dallas wrinkled his nose.

"Pearl!" my sister yelled again. Then, "Mom! Dad!" Before my parents could rush into the room, Lexie had grabbed Snuffy from me and stuffed him into the bag. "You are *so* going to get it," she said in a voice that reminded me of a snake.

"What is going on in here?" asked my father.

"Look what Pearl did!" cried Lexie. Her calm, reasonable voice had vanished. It had been replaced by a more familiar enraged one.

"What?" asked both of my parents. They couldn't see Snuffy since he was back in the bag.

"She made Dallas look at Sn— at my baby blanket!"

Both of my parents turned their eyes on me.

"Pearl," my mother said in a warning voice.

But Lexie interrupted her. Her calm, grown-up tone was back. "Mom, let me talk to her, please. Dallas, will you excuse me?"

Lexie stood up all cool and regal and took me by the hand. She led me into the hall and down to my room. When we were standing inside my doorway, she just looked at me for a moment: Then she said, "I am no longer speaking to you," and left the room, striding away in her purple shoes. I didn't think the silent treatment had been over in the first place, but whatever.

I flopped on my bed. I could feel tears filling up my eyes but I ignored them. Instead I looked through my desk drawers until I found the chart I had made comparing Lexie and me.

I studied it. There was nothing on the chart that was pro me. Not one single pro Pearl item. Lexie was better than me in every way.

That was not right.

I thought and thought and thought.

Finally I added a line at the end:

	☺ LeXie	☺ PeaYl
Stuck up	yes	no

I stared at the new line. It didn't make me feel any better, and I knew why. Because it wasn't true. Lexie was not stuck up. In fact, that was one of the things the Emmas liked about her. I had heard them say so. Furthermore, Lexie had lots of interests. She had won awards for being good in some of her interests, like gymnastics. She was a good student too and mostly got

As and had won awards for citizenship and math, etc., etc., etc. She did all those things and she wasn't stuck up either.

I erased the line from the chart. I wanted the chart to be accurate. But I wouldn't be satisfied until I could be as good as—or better than—Lexie at . . . something.

One evening at the end of September I wandered into the family room and announced, "I'm bored." My parents looked up in alarm. That is not something they like to hear. It makes them nervous. In the past when I've gotten bored I have:

1. given Bitey a haircut
2. given myself a haircut
3. dropped eggs out the kitchen window
4. annoyed Mrs. Mott by barking outside her door

"Bored?" repeated my father. "What have you done?" His eyes jumped to my hair.

"Nothing," I replied. I flopped down between them on the couch. "What are you guys doing?"

Each of my parents was holding a book. "Reading," said my mother.

"Oh."

"Why don't *you* read?" suggested my father.

I shrugged. "I don't like to read."

My parents sighed. "You have so many lovely books," said Mom. And I thought it was nice of her not to point out that I hadn't even read the last one she'd written.

I shrugged again. "Not everyone likes to read."

"How about playing a game?" asked Dad.

I shook my head.

"Do you have any homework?" asked Mom.

I did, but it was Friday. "I'll do it on Sunday," I told her.

My parents glanced at each other.

"What's Lexie doing?" my father wanted to know.

I wasn't sure. I had just walked by her room, and hanging on the closed door I'd seen both the NO PEARL sign and the NO UNDERWEAR VISITS sign (her version). Clearly, I wasn't welcome. "I think she's busy," I said.

"How about starting an art project?" asked my mother.

An art project sounded like fun, but I had another fun idea in mind: a sleepover with Justine. There was just one problem. Since Justine was so young, the last couple of times she'd slept over my mother had ended up walking her back to her own apartment in the middle of the night. The first time it was because Justine had had a bad dream about a bus, and the second time it was because Justine had woken up and couldn't go back to sleep and then she had started to cry because she thought Bitey was in the room (he wasn't), and because she didn't want to eat bekfrixt at our house in the morning. Bekfrixt=breakfast.

I was about to say no to the art project, but suddenly I changed my mind. "Okay!" I said. "That's a good idea. See you later."

I left the family room in a hurry, ran by Lexie's door with all its signs (I could hear her talking on the phone on the other side of it), and made a dash for my art supplies. I keep them in the bottom drawer of my desk. I have markers and paints and colored paper and rubber stamps and inkpads, and a lot of decorations like glitter and sequins and ribbon, and also googly eyes in case I need them for an animal face. I looked through the papers for a minute or two before I finally chose one that was a nice shade of lavender. I folded it in half to make a card. On the outside I stamped a flower over and over with red ink and then I made a border of green glitter around the edges. I drew some bees among the flowers. I added ZZZZZ here and there like the bees were buzzing. When I was satisfied, I opened the card and wrote inside:

Dear Justine,
You are cordally invited to a sleepover.
Where? In my room.
When? Right now.
Why? For fun.
I really really really hope you can come.
Love,
  Your fiend,
    Pearl Littlefield ✿

I put the card in an envelope and tiptoed past the family room. I had almost reached the front door when my father called, "Pearl? What are you up to?"

"Um . . . I'm going to Justine's."

"What's that in your hand?" asked Lexie from behind me.

I jumped. I hadn't heard her door open.

"Nothing." I'm not supposed to invite Justine for sleepovers without checking with my parents first. And I knew they would say no.

"Pearl? What *are* you up to?" asked my father again.

I slid the invitation behind my back. I was about to reach for the doorknob when the telephone rang.

"I'll get it!" I cried, but my father got there first.

"Yes?" he said. Then he frowned. He stood up and began scrabbling through some stuff in the drawer of the telephone table. "Excuse me, can you repeat that?"

"Paul?" asked my mother, and she sounded alarmed.

My father cradled the phone against his ear and whispered, "I need paper and a pen."

Mom ran into her office. While she was gone, Dad sank onto the couch and said, "And the doctor told you what? . . . But how long ago was this? . . . I can be there in an hour or two. . . . You're where now? In the emergency room?"

When I heard the words "emergency room" I began to feel a little scared. I think Lexie did too. She edged toward me until we were standing side by side in the family room. The invitation slipped from my fingers, but no one noticed.

Mom returned with a pad of paper and a pen, and Dad took them and began writing furiously. At last he said, "All right. Thank you so much, Will. I'll see you as soon as I can get there."

Will. I glanced at Lexie. Will was Daddy Bo's neighbor, the one who had gone on the field trip with him. If Will was calling Dad and talking about emergency rooms and doctors . . . I reached for Lexie's hand and she squeezed it.

"Dad?" I said the moment he'd hung up the phone.

Mom and Lexie and I were standing in a line in front of the couch. My father looked at each of us. "That was Will Henderson," he said. "Daddy Bo had a fall a couple of hours ago. He's in the hospital."

"Had a fall?" my mother repeated. "Is—?"

My father interrupted her. "He's going to be all right. He broke his shoulder and he's pretty black and blue, but he managed to call for an ambulance, and Will rode with him to the hospital. They're still in the emergency room. I told Will I'd get there as soon as I can." Dad grabbed his coat and his keys and headed for the door.

"Don't you want to pack a few things?" asked Mom.

Dad shook his head. "I'll be back tomorrow, I'm sure. And I can sleep at my father's if I don't spend the night at the hospital."

This was exciting. Like a show on TV. It was a true and honest emergency.

"I'll call the garage and tell them you're on your way to pick up the car," said Mom.

"Thanks." Dad sprinted into the hall.

I don't remember the last time I saw Dad run, since he's an economics professor and not like the other dads I know, such as Justine's who does something with computers and wears blue jeans and is always going to the gym.

Mom phoned down to the basement of our building, where there's a garage, and that's where we keep our green Subaru. "Sorry to give you such short notice," she said to Raymond, who's in charge of the garage at night, "but Paul's on his way to get the car."

"It's an emergency!" I shouted into the phone, and Mom waved her hand at me.

"He'll be bringing it back tomorrow," she added.

I ran to Justine's and rapped on her door: *knock, knock-knock, knock-knock-knock.* When Justine answered I said, "We have an emergency at my house! Daddy Bo fell and had to go to the hospital in an ambulance, and Dad's driving to New Jersey to meet Will at the hospital. He's not coming back until tomorrow."

Justine's eyes grew large. At first I thought she was impressed with our emergency, but then I saw that Bitey had escaped into the hall and was stalking toward us. "Go home!" I called to Bitey, but cats never listen. "Well, anyway," I said to Justine, who was already bathed and in her nightgown, "I'll talk to you again tomorrow when I know more."

"Okay." Justine closed her door quickly.

I scooped Bitey into my arms and carried him home. The first thing I saw was Justine's invitation lying on the floor. I set Bitey down and threw the invitation away. I didn't need it. I certainly wasn't bored anymore.

"Mom? Can I help you with anything?" I asked.

My mother had just picked up the phone. Probably she needed to make some important calls to inform people of the tragedy. She looked shocked that I had offered to help.

"It's an emergency," I reminded her, "and Dad is gone. I thought you might need help with . . ." Well, I wasn't sure with what, but people always bustle about in these situations, and I wanted to be a part of things.

Mom sat down on the couch with the phone in her hand. "Thank you, Pearl. I appreciate that. Let me see. You could go into my office and get my address book. I need to see if I have Will's cell phone number written down there. Oh, and then you could get the calendar from the kitchen. I may have to cancel a few things this weekend."

"Okay." I felt very important as I collected the address book and the calendar and brought them to Mom. I noticed that Lexie was once again in her room, probably calling all her friends on her own cell phone to tell them what had happened.

"Anything else I can do?" I asked Mom when she had finished with her calls.

"I can't think of anything. Not yet. We need to hear from your father first."

I got ready for bed then. I was just coming out of the bathroom when the phone rang. Mom answered it by saying, "Hi, Paul. Are you already at the hospital?" So I knew it was Dad on his cell phone.

"Daddy Bo is going to be fine," Mom told Lexie and

me later. "He'll stay in the hospital for a few days, but Dad will come home tomorrow. He can fill us in on everything then."

"Whew," said Lexie. "That's a relief."

But I didn't feel like the emergency was over. "Mom, you'll probably need me to sleep with you tonight," I said, "since you'll be lonely without Dad. So don't worry. I'll be there for you." Which was more than Lexie could say.

What she did say, though, was, "Oh, Pearl. When will you outgrow sleeping with Mom and Dad?"

It's true that I do still like to sleep with my parents sometimes, but I thought it was quite rude of Lexie to say so when I was just trying to be nice to Mom. I was about to point out that Lexie had been no help whatsoever all evening, when she said, "Poor Mom. Do you want me to make you a cup of tea?"

Still, I figured I was ahead of Lexie, two to one, in helping Mom cope with the emergency:

> ME—1. Finding her address book and calendar, and 2. offering to sleep with her.
> LEXIE—1. Offering to make her tea.
> (That's all.)

On the other hand, Lexie was ahead of me in everything else in life one hundred billion to approx. zero.

Dad came back the next day, right after lunch. He looked very tired and said he hadn't gotten any sleep the night before.

"Really? You never went to bed at all?" I said.

"He was in a *hos*pital, Pearl," said Lexie.

"Duh. I *know* where he *was*. And hospitals are full of *beds*."

"Yeah. For the *pa*tients."

"Girls," said Mom, and that was all she needed to say.

Dad flopped onto an armchair. His hair was messed up, he had loosened his tie, and his shirttail was sticking out. Also, I am sorry to have to report this, but he smelled a little.

"Wow, Dad." I leaned over and sniffed his shirt.

"Pearl!" shrieked Lexie.

"What?"

"That is so rude!"

Well, Lexie had been rude the night before, so now we were even on rudeness, one to one.

Mom brought Dad a sandwich, and I could hear the coffeemaker start to slurp in the kitchen.

"The thing is," said Dad after he had eaten a few bites of turkey and cheese, and removed Bitey from his lap 4x, "Daddy Bo will be released from the hospital on Wednesday, which is good news, but there's bad news too: He won't be able to care for himself at home. And even when his shoulder is all well I don't think he'll be able to care for himself anymore."

"What? Why?" I asked. Just a few weeks ago Daddy Bo was going on field trips to Philadelphia.

"Will and I had a chance to talk last night, and Will told me some things that concern me. He said he doesn't think Daddy Bo cooks for himself anymore. He just eats frozen dinners or gets takeout. Will isn't sure he's remembering to do his laundry, and he worries because Daddy Bo is unsteady on his feet sometimes. Which is probably how he fell in the first place."

"Where did he fall?" I interrupted. "Was it on the stairs? Did he bleed a lot?"

"Pearl!" exclaimed Lexie again. "Do you have to know every gory detail?"

Well, of course. The gory details are the best ones.

"Excuse me for interrupting," I said primly.

"That's all right." Dad shooed Bitey off of his lap once again. "I wanted to know too."

"See?" I said to Lexie.

"Apparently he slipped getting out of the shower," Dad continued. "I went over to his house today before I came home, and I took a look around. His stairways are dark and so are the halls, and I saw plenty of things he could trip over. What's worse is that everything Will told me seems to be true. There was almost no food in the refrigerator, and there was dirty laundry piled up in the bedroom, not to mention garbage piled up in the kitchen. I'm afraid someday he's going to leave a burner on. I don't know if he remembers to lock his doors, and I don't even want to imagine what he's like behind the wheel of a car."

"He can't live on his own anymore," said Mom quietly.

Dad swallowed a bite of sandwich. Several seconds went by and he cleared his throat. A lot. "No," he said finally. "I don't think he can."

The rest of the afternoon passed slowly. Lexie went off with her keys to the apartment and her cell phone and her friends, Justine and her parents left for the Children's Museum, and Mom and Dad closed themselves into Mom's office to talk. I could think of nothing to do except my homework. One science worksheet, one math worksheet, and use our vocabulary words in sentences. I did the worksheets first, saving the sentences for last since I hate thinking up sentences, which is weird because that is what my mother does all day long. There were ten vocabulary words, and the last one was "habitat," since we were studying habitats in science, but I still couldn't think of any sentence except *Habitat is our number ten vocab. word.*

"There," I said to Bitey, who was sitting on the floor at my feet, tail switching dangerously back and forth. "All done. Want to watch TV with me?" I picked Bitey up, but he bit me so I put him down again. He followed me into the family room, though. I lay on the couch and Bitey lay on my head. I was feeling around for the remote control, trying not to jostle Bitey, when Mom and Dad came into the room, looking serious.

"Is Lexie back yet?" asked Mom.

I started to shake my head, but when Bitey dug his claws into my scalp, I just said, "Nope." Then I added, "I did all my homework."

"That's wonderful!" exclaimed Dad. "Would you like me to check it?"

"Not really," I said, thinking of that tenth sentence.

We all heard the key turn in the lock then, and Bitey, as if he'd heard an explosion instead, leaped off my head, scratching my cheek, and tore into the kitchen at top speed, his nails skittering on the floor.

"Ow," I said.

"Hi," said Lexie.

"I'm glad you're back," said Mom. "Dad and I have been talking and doing a little research this afternoon, and now we need to have a family conference."

Lexie sagged. "A family conference?"

We have family conferences about once a month. Some have been good, such as the one at which Mom and Dad announced that we had a little extra money so we were going to take that trip to Disney World. I hadn't known that the trip would lead to the Show and Tell incident, so it had seemed like a good idea when they'd mentioned it. Even Lexie, who was already twelve then, had jumped up and down and said, "Goody!"

Most of the other conferences, though, have been about chores and responsibilities and manners. I thought this one was probably going to be about the silent treatment plus underwear visits.

"Everyone sit down, please," said Dad, even though I was already sitting down.

I'm glad that at our family conferences all we have to do is talk respectfully. One of Lexie's many friends is a girl named Chloe, and at Chloe's family conferences they pass around this thing called the Talking Stick, and you can only talk when you're holding it, which is supposed to cut down on interrupting. But this is stupid and so is the stick. I saw the stick one day and it's all wrapped in ribbons and has a silver tassel on top to make it look like a fun princess wand instead of what it really is.

Lexie sat next to me on the couch, and Mom and Dad sat across from us in armchairs.

Dad was the first to speak. "This meeting," he began, "is about Daddy Bo. Since he can't go home by himself on Wednesday, Mom and I have decided to bring him here."

"Yes!" I cried, jumping to my feet.

Lexie was smiling.

But Dad looked serious. "There's more. Daddy Bo isn't going to be able to go back to his house. He needs to move to what's called an assisted-living community. Permanently."

"A nursing home?" asked Lexie, and she looked troubled.

"No. Different from a nursing home," spoke up Mom. "Assisted living is for people who are still active but who need help with cooking and cleaning and taking care of themselves. They can still live fairly independently, and they don't need nursing care—"

"But they need assistance?" said Lexie.

"Exactly."

"Is Daddy Bo going to move far away?" I asked.

Mom smiled. "No. That's the good news. There are

several assisted-living facilities very close by. The one we like the best is on the Upper West Side. But every place has a waiting list, and some are quite long. Daddy Bo will need to live with us for at least several months before he can move to a new home."

"Yippee!" I said.

"And while he's here, he'll need a room of his own."

"A room of his own here at our apartment?" asked Lexie suspiciously.

Dad nodded. "So we've decided that Daddy Bo will move into Pearl's room and Pearl will move in with you, Lexie."

My sister shot to her feet as fast as Bitey had leaped off my head. "WHAT?"

"Now calm down," said Mom.

"No way!" exclaimed Lexie. "There is NO way Pearl is moving into my room."

I smiled sweetly. "I would be happy to help out by moving into Lexie's room."

"Thank you," said Dad.

Lexie was still standing, hands on hips. "No way," she said again.

"All right," my mother replied. "There is one other possible solution."

"Anything," muttered Lexie as she flopped back onto the couch, this time a little farther away from me.

"If you don't want Pearl to move into your room, then you can move in with Pearl. It will be a bit tighter, though. Pearl's room is smaller than yours."

Yeah, I thought.

"And Pearl doesn't have bunk beds like you do," added Dad.

Yeah, I thought.

Of course Lexie was on her feet again in one half of a second. "Move into *Pearl's* room?" she cried. She might as well have said, "Move into a *sewer?*"

"Hey! What's wrong with my room?" I asked.

And Dad said, "Lexie, please consider your words. You aren't being very respectful to Pearl."

"Sorry," muttered Lexie as she sat down again.

Mom clapped her hands together. "Those are the two choices," she said decisively. "Daddy Bo needs a space of his own. He can't sleep in the family room—and neither can you or Pearl," she added quickly, seeing the hopeful look on Lexie's face. "There's absolutely no reason the two of you can't share a room. It will only be for a few months. So either Pearl, you move in with Lexie, or Lexie, you move in with Pearl. You girls can decide."

"I'd be very happy with either choice," I said, ignoring Lexie's scowl. Although the truth was, that while it would be fine if Lexie moved into my room, I really, really, really, really, really, really, really wanted to move into hers. I hardly ever even got to *see* inside her room. The door was usually closed and those signs were usually hanging. Here was my chance to *live* in her room. To observe my big sister up close, as if Lexie were an animal in the woods and I were a nature specialist with a fancy camera.

Mom and Dad looked at Lexie. "Well?" said Dad.

Lexie let out a sigh that Justine could have heard if she'd been at home. "Okay. Pearl can move into my room."

"Thank you," said Mom and Dad.

Thank you, thank you, thank you, thank you, thank you! I thought. Soon I would be inside the magic lair of Lexie Littlefield.

"But I'm not happy about this," declared Lexie, and she flumped out of the family room, down the hall, and into her room.

She closed her door with just a bit too much force.

I smiled and stood up. "I think I'll go make Daddy Bo a get-well card," I said. I was feeling inspired.

I sat at my desk with a sheet of white paper before me. I thought for a long time before I drew a picture of a man lying in a hospital bed with a big cast on his foot and his leg in traction. I knew Daddy Bo had broken his shoulder, not his leg, but I really wanted to write inside the card:

Dear Daddy Bo,
    Here's hoping you're back on your feet soon!!!

                    Love, Pearl Littlefield

On the way to the family room to show the card to Mom and Dad, I paused outside Lexie's door. Soon I would be on the other side of it, sleeping on the bunk bed, watching Lexie choose her outfits, and listening to her phone conversations with her friends.

These were probably going to be the best months of my life.

"I advise you to be careful." That was pretty much the first thing Lexie said to me on Sunday, and she said it at 3:00 p.m. in the afternoon, so you can see that the silent treatment had been back in place.

Advise. Like Lexie was a warning label.

"You're not being very respectful, Lexie," I replied.

My sister sighed. "I'm just saying to be careful."

"I'm *try*ing." I was trying to have fun too, since here I was moving into Lexie's room three days early. Mom and Dad had decided at breakfast that the move should take place right away, since we had the whole day free and they would both be around to help out.

"Yippee!" I had said.

But Lexie had hung her head so low that her hair

drooped into her Cheerios a little bit and she'd given me a dirty look as she wiped the milk off.

I didn't care. I had just been granted three extra days inside Lexie's room. I spent the morning taking all my clothes out of my dresser and closet and piling them on the bed, and then emptying the drawers of my desk and the shelves of my bookcase. When I was done, the edges of my room were bare, and the middle part looked like the Lost and Found bin at school.

"Good heavens," Mom had said at lunchtime when she'd poked her head into my room to check on my progress. "Maybe you ought to take advantage of the situation and do a little cleaning out."

I was in such a good mood that I had agreed without arguing, and I got a large garbage bag from under the kitchen sink and threw away quite a lot of things, such as the leaf shaped like a fish that I'd found in Central Park, and a doll whose arm had fallen off and gotten lost, and a package of dried-up markers, and also a moldy plum, which I didn't mention to anyone. Then I cleaned out my clothes and made up a bag of things that would fit Justine soon.

"Good job, Pearl," said Mom.

But when Lexie had peeked around my door later and had seen how much stuff was still left she wailed, "There's no way all of *that* is going to fit in my room!"

Mom and Dad agreed with her. "You don't have to

move *every*thing out," Dad told me. "Daddy Bo won't need too much space."

"Why won't he?" I asked. "He has a whole house full of stuff."

"Yes, but we're not going to bring all of it to the apartment. And even when Daddy Bo moves to a new place he'll only have a few rooms, so he'll need his clothes and books and a few pieces of furniture, but not much more."

I'd realized that although my father didn't smell today, he still looked tired, and a couple of times that morning he hadn't heard me when I was talking to him and I'd had to repeat myself until the words started to sink in and then he was like, "What? What?" And that was how I knew he was worried about Daddy Bo.

"What are you going to do with the rest of Daddy Bo's stuff?" Lexie wanted to know now.

"Put it in storage for the time being," Mom replied. "When he's feeling better we'll talk to him about it."

"So how much space should I clear for him?" I asked, looking around my room.

"How about," said Dad, "two of your dresser drawers, two of your shelves, and half of your closet?"

"Okay," I replied.

"Thank you for being so cooperative, Pearl."

"You're welcome."

"And Lexie," Dad continued, "can you clear out

two drawers, two shelves, and half of your closet for Pearl?"

"I'm not sure how . . ."

Dad gave her a Look, which meant he was feeling impatient, which was probably due to his tiredness.

"But I'll figure something out."

"Thank you."

I noticed my father hadn't said, "Thank you for being so cooperative, Lexie."

So I had put back some of my things, leaving plenty of space for Daddy Bo, and now, at long last, I was actually moving into Lexie's room. And I was trying to have fun. But I knocked the edge of a carton against Lexie's desk and this was when she advised me to be careful, and I told her she wasn't being respectful, and she said she was *just saying* to be careful, etc., etc., etc., and so forth.

I left the carton on her floor, and returned to my room for another load, then hurried back through her door, which Mom and Dad had told her she had to leave open, and dumped an armload of clothes on the floor.

"Dresser," commanded Lexie, pointing to the dresser as if maybe I wasn't old enough to identify furniture.

"Which are my drawers?" I asked. I knew better than to pull them open to find out for myself.

"The bottom two."

At least the silent treatment had ended.

I opened the drawers and began shoving my clothes inside. When I was finished, I went back to my room and returned with an armful of things from my closet, still on their hangers.

"Which half of the closet?" I asked.

Lexie was lying on the top bunk, gazing down at me like the lazy grasshopper in the fable, not offering to do any work at all.

"The left side."

I hung up the clothes, careful not to let my purple shirt, which was at the right end of my things, touch Lexie's white blouse, which was at the left end of her things. I didn't want to hear a word about germs (mine).

I worked hard all afternoon, carrying my stuff into Lexie's room and arranging everything as neatly as possible. There's no question that we were cramped. The shelves were overflowing, and most of the dresser drawers wouldn't close all the way. The closet door wouldn't close either because apart from our clothes and shoes, we had stuffed stray books and games and even Lexie's old dollhouse into the closet. A lot of my things were under the bottom bunk, and Lexie's violin and violin stand had been moved into the family room, even though she said she was incapable of practicing where people could hear her.

"We can hear you when you practice in your room with the door closed," I told her, and she rolled her eyes.

"Speaking of which," I went on, "you'll have to take down the NO PEARL sign now. You can't forbid me to come in my own room."

"It isn't your—," Lexie started to say, but thought better of it. Instead she grumped over to her door and ripped the sign off. "Happy now?" She glared at me. "And don't ask me to take down the other sign. This room is still at least half mine and I have some rules for living in it. One of them is being fully clothed. Period. End of discussion."

At dinnertime I said, "It's going to be weird not to sleep in my own bed tonight."

Lexie narrowed her eyes at me. "Why won't you sleep in your own bed tonight?"

"Hello. I just moved into your room."

"But Daddy Bo isn't here yet," said Lexie. "You're not sleeping in my room until he gets here."

"But my underwear is in your dresser! Do you want me coming into your room naked to get my underwear tomorrow?"

"You can put your school clothes in your room tonight," said Lexie, "and get dressed there tomorrow morning after you wake up in your own bed."

My mother cleared her throat. "Actually, Lexie, your father and I cleaned Pearl's room this afternoon and made up the bed for Daddy Bo. So Pearl is now officially your roommate."

"Yes!" I cried.

For once my sister was speechless.

When dinner was over, Lexie went to her room to finish her homework. She sat at her desk with her algebra book open in front of her, which I'm not really sure what algebra is. I lay on my back on the bottom bunk, my knees bent, and pretended my legs were a sliding board for the seven stuffed animals I had moved into my new bedroom. "Whee!" I said as Owlie slid onto my feet. "Wahoo!" I said as Mr. Cougar tumbled off my legs and onto the floor.

"Pearl," said Lexie.

"Yes?"

Lexie sighed. "When I say 'Pearl' like that what it means is, 'Could you please be quiet so I can concentrate?'"

"It would be more helpful if you just said what you meant."

"Could you please be quiet so I can concentrate?"

"Okay." I retrieved Mr. Cougar from the floor. "Whee," I whispered.

Lexie whipped her head around. "I can still hear you. And I'm studying for a test." She stood up, stepped into the hallway, then turned back to me. "I see that we're going to have to establish some rules for homework, and also for privacy. Mom? Dad?" she called.

Half an hour later there were a couple of new rules in place. The first was that I had to respect Lexie's need for silence while studying. (Mom and Dad reminded me that I didn't have to spend *all* my time in my new bedroom. There was still the family room.) The second rule was that Lexie and I were each to have one hour of "alone time" in her room every day, and neither of us could disturb the other until the hour was up. My hour was to be in the afternoon, Lexie's was to be after dinner. I had a feeling that all the good phone calls and things were going to take place during Lexie's alone time, but there wasn't anything I could do about it.

"I'm not going to need my alone time," I announced to Lexie.

"What?" Lexie murmured.

"I *said*, I'm not going to need my alone time."

Lexie and I were in the bunk beds, settled in for our first night as roommates. There was no reply from above.

"Lexie?"

"*What?*"

"I said—"

"I know what you said. I'm trying to read."

I perched Owlie on Mr. Cougar's back. "Don't you want to know why I won't need my alone time? . . . Lexie?"

"WHAT?"

"Don't you want to know why I won't need my alone time?"

"No."

"It's because I don't need any privacy."

"Pearl, don't you have something to read?"

"Nope."

"Not a single thing?"

"I left my books in the other room."

"So go get one."

"That's okay."

"Then read something of mine."

"No, thank you."

"Then be quiet so I can read."

I lay in my bed in silence until I began to feel sleepy. I wondered how long it would take for Lexie to discover the new sign on her door.

On Monday morning Lexie's alarm clock went off and she slung back her covers in a flash. She scrambled down the ladder, opened the door to our room, and saw the new sign.

"What is this, may I ask?" She held out the PEARL'S ROOM sign, which she had ripped off the door.

"I made it," I replied from the bottom bunk. "Do you like it?"

My sister didn't answer. She dropped it in the wastebasket.

"Lexie?" I said. "How come you're so mean to me?"

She paused. Then she sat on the edge of my bed and sighed. "Pearl, I don't like being mean to you, but let's see. You hide my shoes—for sport. You show my baby blanket to my boyfriend. You scare me for no good reason. And those are just some of the things you've done recently. Really, Pearl, what do you expect?"

"I don't know," I mumbled.

Lexie stood up. "I'll use the bathroom now," she said, "and you can get dressed. Then you can use the bathroom while I get dressed, okay?"

"Okay. Lexie, could you take down the other sign? Please? It would only be fair. I know this isn't my room, not entirely, so my sign was wrong. But this is half my room, at least for a while, and you can't make me promise that I'll *always* be fully clothed in here. I might have to wear just my underwear sometimes. In fact, I'm going to be in my underwear in a few minutes, while I'm getting dressed."

"Okay," said Lexie. "You're right. Fair enough." She took down the NO UNDERWEAR VISITS sign and threw it away with the other ones.

On Tuesday afternoon just before my alone time was supposed to begin, I said, "Lexie, I really don't need my hour." (I hadn't needed it the day before, either.) "So you can come in if you want."

"That's okay," Lexie replied. "I'm going to practice my violin out here." She was standing in the family room. "It's nice and quiet, I have plenty of space, and I still won't have an audience."

"How come you don't like audiences? If you

become a violin player, won't you want people to hear you?"

"I'll want them to hear me play, not practice. I like to make mistakes in private."

"Lexie?" I said. (I wasn't done talking.) "I think we should give Daddy Bo presents. To welcome him to his new home."

Lexie arranged some sheet music on the stand. "I already made one for him," she said. She stuck the violin under her chin.

"So did I! What did you make?"

"A scarf. I finished knitting it last night."

"Oh."

"What did you make him?"

"A map."

Lexie lowered the violin. "A map of what?"

"Our apartment building."

Lexie started to snort but turned it into a laugh. "Why does he need a map of our apartment building?"

"So he won't get lost, duh."

"Tone of voice, Pearl!" called my mother from her office. How had she heard me with the door closed?

"What I meant," I said to Lexie, "is that Daddy Bo hasn't been here in a while, and anyway, he's never *lived* here, so he might not know where certain things are, like Justine's apartment or the laundry room or the storage units or the mailboxes. Oh, or that room people keep their bicycles in." I stopped talking when I saw the look on my sister's face. "And before you say anything, I know Daddy Bo doesn't have a bike and plus he broke his shoulder, but he might need to know where the bike room is sometime. For some reason."

Lexie laid her violin in its case. "Can I see the map?" she asked.

I retrieved it from my notebook, which I had jammed under my new bed.

Lexie looked and looked at the map, but her eyes didn't give away her personal, private opinions. Finally she said, "I can tell you put a lot of thought into this, Pearl." She sounded like Mr. Potter when he wasn't sure what to say about something, such as once when Jill spent forever making a painting in art class and no one, including Rachel and Katie, could figure out what it was a drawing *of*. Mr. Potter had leaned over Jill's shoulder then and said, "I love all the colors you used—and there's so much *energy* here!"

Still, when Lexie said she could tell I had put a lot of thought into the map I kind of believed her, and I felt proud.

Lexie folded her handmade three-color scarf into a box, which she wrapped in striped paper, and I rolled up the map and tied it with a green ribbon. We were ready for Daddy Bo.

✦✳✦

He arrived the next afternoon. Dad had skipped work that day and had driven to New Jersey, gone to Daddy Bo's house, and packed up some of his stuff, then rushed over to the hospital, where he'd collected Daddy Bo. He and Daddy Bo and the stuff arrived at our apartment late in the afternoon.

I was in the family room with Lexie and Bitey when I heard the key in the lock. "They're here!" I shouted, and Bitey skittered behind the couch.

The door swung open and there stood Dad and Daddy Bo. Puffing in the hallway behind them was Reginald, who's the porter in our building, which means he lugs stuff around for you if you need help. Reginald, who was sweating in addition to puffing, was pulling along a very rattly metal cart, and piled on the cart were three suitcases and two cardboard boxes.

"Daddy Bo!" I shrieked.

"Daddy Bo!" called Lexie.

"Mom, Daddy Bo's here!" I yelled.

"So I hear," said Mom, who as it turned out, was standing right behind me.

I took a good look at Daddy Bo, half hoping for bruises and bandages and stitches, which would have made his accident even more interesting, but all I saw was a white sling keeping his shoulder in place.

"Where's your cast?" I asked him.

"Pearl!" hissed Lexie. And I knew this was another of

those times when "Pearl" meant a whole lot more than just my name. This afternoon I think it meant, "Quit being so nosy." I think it also meant, "You're embarrassing me," and I could see why she didn't want to say that out loud.

But Daddy Bo didn't seem to mind my question. "No cast," he replied. "Isn't that boring?"

"Oh, well," I said. I started to fling myself at Daddy Bo, but Mom pulled me back.

"Careful," she said. "No hugging for a while. I'll bet Daddy Bo is pretty sore."

Daddy Bo gave us a sad smile. "Sore isn't the word."

"What is the word?" I wanted to know.

"That's just an expression, Pearl," said Lexie. Then she stepped forward and helped Daddy Bo remove his coat.

This is the nice thing about my sister. She might not have wanted me to move into her room, but she also didn't want Daddy Bo to think he was causing any trouble. She loves Daddy Bo as much as I do.

We walked slowly into the family room then. Lexie held Daddy Bo's uninjured arm and I patted his back while he shuffled along, moving about one half of an inch at a time. Behind us, Mom and Dad helped Reginald unload the cart, and then Reginald and the empty cart disappeared onto the service elevator.

"Sit right here," I instructed Daddy Bo. "This chair is the most comfortable seat in the whole apartment."

"Thank you, Pearl," he replied. "You're a gem."

The first time Daddy Bo had said that to me I hadn't understood the joke. So Lexie had explained it to me and then I'd told it to Justine, but she'd remained mystified, even after *I'd* explained it to her twice.

"Hey, careful!" Lexie exclaimed, as Daddy Bo lost his balance and pretty much fell into the chair.

"Lawsy," said Daddy Bo. "First day with my new feet."

Daddy Bo was breathing hard, and I glanced nervously at Lexie. Then I looked around for Mom and Dad, but they were wrestling the suitcases and cartons down the hallway to my old room.

Lexie glanced back at me. After a few moments while we stood uncertainly over Daddy Bo, listening to him try to catch his breath, Lexie said brightly, "We made presents for you!"

"For me? How nice," said Daddy Bo. "I certainly am lucky."

"If you were really lucky you probably wouldn't have fallen," I told him.

Lexie glared at me, but Daddy Bo started to laugh. "True enough," he replied.

I retrieved Daddy Bo's presents from where I had hidden them, which was behind the couch. Bitey had been sitting on Lexie's gift and I hoped she wouldn't notice the dent and all the gray fur. She did, but she didn't say anything. She just handed the box to Daddy Bo. When he opened it he exclaimed, "Fabulous! This will keep my neck extra warm. I can't believe you made it yourself. Thank you, Lexie."

"Now mine! Open mine!" I said. I hopped back and forth from one foot to the other.

Daddy Bo slid the ribbon off of the map and unrolled it.

"It's a map of the apartment building!" I announced as he studied it. "Now you'll know where everything is around here."

"This will come in very handy," he said seriously. "I had no idea there was a bike room in the basement."

I looked triumphantly at my sister, who ignored me and pretended to be all adult by saying, "Daddy Bo, would you like to settle into your new room now?"

"Thank you, but I need a moment to collect myself."

"While you're doing that, could I sit in your lap?" I asked. "I'll be very careful, I promise."

"Sure," said Daddy Bo.

So I settled into his lap, leaning gingerly against his good shoulder. After a moment I couldn't help myself: I poked his double chin, making it sway back and forth. "What's this for?" I said, like I always did.

Daddy Bo smiled. "I was wondering when you'd ask," he replied. "That's where old people keep their pills."

I sat in Daddy Bo's lap for a long time while he wore his scarf and consulted his map and we listened to Lexie play (not practice) her violin.

10

My grandmother (not Daddy Bo's wife, who's dead, but my other grandmother) once said to Lexie and me, "You poor babies. Growing up in the city. You don't even get to see the seasons change." Well, obviously, that grandmother had not spent much time in the city. Because for instance, today, which was a Saturday in early autumn, I could see red and yellow leaves swirling around outside our windows. And I could hear the wind blowing a little. And when I looked down onto the street I could see that people were wearing jackets. Also I could see that LaVerne, the woman who owns the hot chestnut cart, was wheeling it toward Fifth Avenue. I have to be honest and tell you that hot chestnuts actually taste like hot bars of soap, but I like LaVerne, and her cart was a true sign of autumn.

Since it was the weekend, I was wearing my pirate outfit. I had spruced it up, but not with a hook hand, which Mom and Dad still refused to buy me. Instead I had spruced it up by tying a checkered scarf around my neck. And I had decided to make a flag with a skull and crossbones on it.

I worked busily on the flag, sitting at the table in the family room and painting a square of black fabric. Daddy Bo was reading the paper on the couch. He had been with us for over two weeks and his shoulder was much better. He was still wearing the sling, but he could move around more and I didn't have to be so careful when I climbed in his lap to poke his chin.

"Isn't this a nice day?" I said to Daddy Bo as I dabbed white paint onto the black cotton.

"It's a gem of a day, Pearl."

"I don't have any homework."

"Neither do I."

I smiled. "And we don't have to go anywhere or do anything unless we feel like it. This is the best kind of day ever."

The doorbell rang then and I ran to answer it.

"Hi, Pearl," said Valerie, stepping inside. "Is Lexie here?"

"Yup!" said Lexie, rushing to the front door. "Here I am! Hi, Valerie! I didn't know you were coming over."

"I was wondering if you wanted to go to the park and watch the boys' soccer team practice," said Valerie. "Polly just called and she and Chloe are already on their way over there."

"Oh, Lexie, too bad. You can't go," I said.

"She can't? Why not?" asked Valerie.

"Because last night she threw up. In her bed."

Lexie's face turned a very bright shade of pink. "I did not!" she yelped. "I did not throw up in my bed!"

"Yes, you did." I turned to Valerie. "She really did. A little bit before she got to the bathroom. I heard her. And I saw Mom take the blanket off her bed. There was definitely throw-up on it."

"You must have been dreaming, Pearl," said Lexie, but her face was as pink as ever.

Valerie looked questioningly at Lexie, who looked furiously at me. My sister reminded me a little of Mrs. Mott when she catches people riding on the regular elevator with their dogs.

"Are you okay?" Valerie asked Lexie.

"I'm fine now. Do I look sick?"

Lexie actually did not look sick. She was dressed and she was eating a pear.

"I guess not," said Valerie.

Lexie shrugged into her coat, grabbed her purse, and put her cell phone in it. "Mom!" she shouted. "Dad! I'm going to the park with Valerie!"

Ten minutes after Lexie left, my parents announced that they were going to run errands.

"We'll be gone for about an hour," said Dad.

Since they hadn't run errands in quite some time, I knew they would actually be gone for about three hours.

"Can you two take care of each other?" Mom asked Daddy Bo and me.

I looked at my grandfather and grinned. "Don't worry about us," I said.

My parents left and I studied the skull I had painted and decided to make its eye sockets red. I was admiring my work when I realized that Daddy Bo wasn't sitting on the couch anymore. He was standing by the window, staring outside.

"Did you finish the paper?" I asked him.

"Cover to cover."

"What are you going to do now?"

"I don't know. What are you going to do?"

I wasn't finished with the flag, but I set it aside and said, "Do you want to play a game or something?"

"Sure," replied Daddy Bo.

I opened the closet where we keep some of our toys and pulled out Sorry! It is currently my favorite game. My favorite game used to be Mouse Trap, but I have moved beyond that.

I arranged the Sorry! board and cards and game pieces on the table.

"Have you ever played this before?" I asked Daddy Bo.

He looked uncertain. "A long time ago, I think. I might need a refresher course before we start."

"Okay. Well, it's a little like Parcheesi. You have four pieces, and the object of the game is to get all of them around the board from your starting point to your home. And you do that by drawing these cards." I indicated the pile of cards in the middle of the board.

"No dice?" asked Daddy Bo.

"No dice. Each card has a number on it, and each number means something different. Like, for instance, a four means you have to move one of your pieces *backward* four spaces. And if you draw a seven, you can split the move between two of your pieces. You could move one five spaces and another two spaces. Now if you draw an eleven, you can move forward eleven, *or* switch places with another player's piece. That could get one of your pieces almost Home, and send the other player's way back, depending on where the pieces are on the board."

"Very tricky," said Daddy Bo. "Also, a little hard to remember."

"I'll remind you," I offered. "I'm sort of a professional. Now, what color do you want to be?"

Daddy Bo chose green, which was good, since I always like to be red. But if he had chosen red I wouldn't have said anything.

I let him go first. "You have to draw a one or a two to get your pieces moving," I said.

Daddy Bo drew a four and hopped one of his pieces four spaces around the board.

"Um," I said, "you have to draw a *one* or a *two* before you can start. And anyway, four goes backward."

"Oh, dear." Daddy Bo returned his piece to Start and scratched his head.

"My turn," I said, and drew a two and got going.

Then Daddy Bo drew a one and looked at me.

"Okay, now you can go!"

He edged one of his pieces onto the board.

I drew a twelve, which is a very good card, and I slid a long way around the board.

Daddy Bo studied his fingernails.

"Your turn."

"Oh." Daddy Bo's next card was a five. "Drat," he said.

"No, that's okay. You can move that piece five spaces." I pointed to the one that had moved one space on his last turn.

"Huh." Daddy Bo's gaze had drifted to the window.

"Don't you want to play?" I asked.

"Oh, sure."

But each time Daddy Bo drew a card I had to tell him what to do. It was like playing Sorry! with Justine—or against myself, which I have tried, and I am here to tell you that it really isn't any fun, because no matter what, you're going to both win and lose every game.

"Daddy Bo, is something wrong?" I finally asked him.

He reached into his pocket. "I can't find my keys."

This was mystifying. I was pretty sure that my father had taken Daddy Bo's keys since Daddy Bo didn't need them anymore. He lived with us now, and his car and his house were back in New Jersey.

"What do you mean?" I asked, and then I remembered that my parents had given Daddy Bo a key to the apartment and a key to our mailbox in the lobby. "Oh! Your new keys. I think they're on the table in the hall."

"No, I do not mean any new keys," said Daddy Bo in a tone of voice that reminded me of Lexie. "I mean my old regular keys. The ones on my old regular key ring. They aren't in my pocket and they aren't on my dresser."

"Are you sure you still have those keys?" I said. "Because you don't really need them right now." I was going to say something about his house and his car, but I thought better of it.

"Well . . ." Daddy Bo scratched his head again.

"At least you *have* keys," I said, handing him the new set. "I don't have any keys at all. I don't even have my own key to the apartment. I'm the only one in the family without keys. I don't have a computer or a cell phone either," I added. "But you know who does have those things? Lexie."

I wasn't sure whether Daddy Bo had heard me. He was walking around the family room, peeking in knick-knacks and vases, looking under piles of papers and mail. He ambled back to the window, stared outside again for a few moments, then crossed to the table and began to lift my flag.

"Wait, Daddy Bo! That's still wet!" I cried. I took it from him gently. I was about to say, "Maybe I'd better let it dry in my room," when I remembered that there wasn't an inch of spare space in my new bedroom for drying pirate flags. I laid it on the kitchen counter instead.

"Well, drat!" I heard Daddy Bo say from the family room.

"What is it?" I asked, hurrying through the hallway and tripping over Bitey.

"I can't find my keys," said Daddy Bo again.

I thought for a moment. "Why do you want them?" I asked, and even before Daddy Bo could reply, I knew the answer. It came to me suddenly, and it was the reason *I* wanted keys: If you had been entrusted with keys it meant you were responsible enough to take care of things that were worth locking up, like a house or a car. Or an apartment. Furthermore, keys gave you independence. Daddy Bo had keys now, of course, but he'd been demoted to a mailbox key, and the key to a place where he was only going to live temporarily. The keys to the much more important things in his life—his very own house and his very own car—were gone. And so was his independence.

The fact that I personally would have settled for something as lowly as a mailbox key was kind of pathetic, and the comparison chart flashed into my brain, but I banished the thought of it quickly.

"Daddy Bo," I said, "I think you need a cup of tea."

Mom and Dad came back in just under three hours, and Lexie came back not long after that. The moment she had taken off her coat she grabbed my arm and pulled me into our bedroom.

"Pearl," she said, and she looked around the room but didn't see any place where the two of us could sit down together except on the floor, so she shoved aside a pile of books, and Owlie and Mr. Cougar, who had fallen out of bed, and hauled me down next to her. "I didn't want to say anything before because I was too mad and anyway Valerie was here, but I'm going to say it now."

"Are you still mad?" I asked, thinking that she'd had several hours in which to cool off. She could have counted to ten about 1,000x since she'd huffed off with her best friend.

"Yes. I am still mad. Pearl, you had no right to tell Valerie what happened last night. You wouldn't even have known about it if you weren't sharing my room. And anyway, it wasn't your news to tell, since it happened to me."

I tried to think of a nice way to ask my question. "So you admit that it happened?"

Lexie glared at me. "You are so rude!"

I hadn't meant to be rude. I just really wanted to know if I was right.

"Out!" cried Lexie, and she pointed to the door as if I were a puppy she was training, except that she was using a very mean tone of voice for either a puppy or a sister.

I started to stomp out of the room, but then I turned back and grabbed something from one of my two drawers.

"What's that?" asked Lexie.

"None of your business." I started to stomp down the hall, but saw that the door to my old room was closed. Daddy Bo was taking a nap. I stomped back into Lexie's room. "I need my alone time," I announced. "*You* go out!"

Lexie was so surprised that she stood up without asking any questions and left me alone. I closed the door quietly and sat at Lexie's desk with the comparison chart in front of me. I added a new line:

	☺ Lexie	☺ Pearl
Has Thrown Up in Own Bed	yes	no

At last something I could be proud of.

11

After I added the new line to the chart, I looked at my watch. One minute had gone by. I had fifty-nine minutes of alone time left. And since I had made such a big deal out of needing it, I realized I'd better use up the whole hour. I knew I couldn't snoop through Lexie's things. Mom and Dad had been clear about the rules of alone time. So I stretched out on the bottom bunk with Owlie on my stomach and I said to him, "Do you understand Lexie?" I said it very quietly in case my sister was eavesdropping in the hall. Then, just to be on the safe side, I tiptoed across the room, knelt down, and peered through the crack under the door to see if Lexie's purple shoes were there. They weren't, but Bitey's feet were, so I let him inside, closed the door, and returned to my bed. Bitey lay down beside me and purred.

I looked at my watch again. Fifty-eight minutes of alone time left. I decided that I might as well spend the rest of the hour doing something useful. "What's the most useful thing I could do?" I asked Bitey, who closed his eyes and covered them with one front paw. "Well, I have the answer, whether you're interested in it or not," I told him.

I needed to figure out how to live with Lexie without annoying her, so I started a list and I titled it Ten Rules For Living With My Sister.

Ten seemed like a nice number, and I was pretty sure I could come up with that many rules. After all, the more rules I had, the more useful the list would be.

The first few rules came to me easily. I could stop playing tricks on Lexie and teasing her, since I knew ahead of time that she would get annoyed. I wrote:

1. Do not hide Lexie's shoes even if you think it's funny.
2. Do not ever let Justine yell Fire!!!!! outside Lexie's door unless there really is a fire.
3. Try not to tease Lexie, sometimes this is hard because she says stupid things.

"But what about all the things I do that I *don't* know are going to annoy her?" I asked. (I was talking to Owlie since Bitey plainly wasn't interested.) I thought over the lessons I had learned in the past few weeks and added another few items to the list:

4. No underwear visits.
5. Don't show Lexie's boyfriend her baby blanket.
6. Don't talk about her throw-up.

I looked at my rules. They were fine, but they were awfully specific. I wasn't sure how much help they'd be in the future. Obviously, I already knew enough not to yell Fire or talk about Lexie's throw-up in front of Valerie. So instead of thinking about myself and what I was doing wrong, I began to think about my sister and her baffling behavior. I realized that the things most likely to make Lexie throw a fit were not listening to her, not taking her seriously, and embarrassing her. I added two more items to the list:

7. Listen to what Lexie says, I mean really listen and then pay attention. It's important to pay attention.
8. Take her seriously. She has no sense of humor about herself and everything embarrasses her.

Now I was getting somewhere. I was rather proud of myself. I thought for a very long time before I finished the list with:

> 9. Try to be more patient with Lexie like Mom and Dad are patient with you.
> 10. It couldn't hurt to tell her you want to be just like her one day, whether you mean it or not.

Good. This was a good list. Plus, the hour would be over in twelve minutes. I slid the list of rules into my drawer along with the comparison chart. I was ready to face Lexie with a new attitude.

It was at dinnertime that night that I got my first chance to use the rules. I was inspecting my macaroni and cheese to make sure it didn't have parsley flakes or anything else that was green in it when Lexie announced, "I have decided that I'm too old to go trick-or-treating this year."

What I wanted to say back to her was, "Are you kidding? You're thirteen, not eighty-five," but I thought that might be mean to Daddy Bo, and then anyway I remembered Rule #8. Next I wanted to say, "But you always go trick-or-treating with me! Why are you doing this? You're just being mean." I remembered Rule #9, though, and kept my mouth shut.

I noticed Lexie looking at me in a funny way, like maybe she wanted to ask me a question, but she didn't.

"Speaking of Halloween," I said after a few moments had gone by, "would you help me with my costume, Daddy Bo?"

Daddy Bo grinned, and his chin swayed a little. "I would be honored," he replied. "Costumes are the best part of Halloween. Have you decided what you want to be this year?"

"I was thinking about a molar," I said, and Daddy Bo's eyes widened. "But don't worry, this other kid in my class, James Brubaker the Third—he lives across the street—well, he's going to be a molar and I don't want anyone to say I copied him, so the tooth's out." (Everyone at the table laughed for some reason, but I ignored them.) "Now my list is down to four things: a miniature pony, a cell phone"—I looked pointedly at my parents—"a drama queen, and Clara Barton."

"The nurse?" asked Daddy Bo.

"The founder of the Red Cross. She lived in colonial times. I think."

"That's quite a list, Pearl," said Mom.

"How would anyone know if you were a miniature pony or a regular one?" asked Lexie, snickering.

Maybe I should make a list of rules for living with *me* and give it to my sister.

"Whatever you decide," said Daddy Bo, "I'll be happy to help you."

"Thank you." I folded my napkin into a tidy rectangle, glanced in Lexie's direction, and then said, "I wonder who will take Justine and me trick-or-treating this year. I mean, since Lexie will be staying home."

Daddy Bo raised his hand like he was in school. "How about your old granddad?"

"Goody!" I said. "Is that okay?" I asked my parents, and they nodded. "It's really fun," I told Daddy Bo. "Justine always comes with me and we go to all the apartments in the building. Every single one. We each get a whole bag full of candy."

"Imagine that," said Daddy Bo.

At dinner the next evening I said, "I decided what I'm going to be for Halloween. A hamster."

"That wasn't even on your list," said Lexie, and she started to laugh, but in a nice way.

The day after that I said, "I changed my mind. I'm going to be a molar after all."

"Uh-oh," said Daddy Bo.

The day after that I said, "I changed my mind again."

"Thank goodness," said Daddy Bo.

"I'm going to be a pirate."

"Oh!" exclaimed Lexie. "That's perfect! You already have such a good costume."

"It could use a little work, though," I said. Then I remembered to add, "Thank you," since my sister had nicely complimented me.

"What else does it need?" asked Lexie.

"A flag. But I'm almost done with the one I was making, so that's taken care of. And a bag for pieces of eight. And a few more scarves and a big earring. And, oh, a hook hand."

My father looked up from his dinner. "I think we could buy you the hook hand now."

"Really? Oh, thank you! Daddy Bo and I can take care of the other things. We can either borrow them or make them. Mom, do you have any scarves you don't want?"

By the week before Halloween my costume was in excellent shape. Daddy Bo had helped me with all sorts of piratey touches, like striped stockings and a medallion to hang around my neck. The hook hand was the best part, though, and I even wrote Mom and Dad a thank-you note for it.

On Sunday afternoon Daddy Bo and I were working on a treasure map that I could attach to the hook, when Lexie wandered into the family room, threw herself dramatically on the couch, and said, "Well, if

I'm going to make a Halloween costume, I'd better get started."

I looked up from my markers. "Why do you need a costume?" My heart began to pound. Lexie must have changed her mind. My big sister was going to go trick-or-treating after all.

"I thought I'd wear it while I hand out candy."

I let out my breath. "You're going to hand out our candy this year?"

"Yup," said Lexie.

Handing out candy sounded even more grownup than deciding not to trick-or-treat.

Halloween was on Thursday. On Wednesday, while Lexie was walking Justine and me home from school, she said, "Hey, you guys, I was wondering—would you like *me* to take you around the building tomorrow?"

"Take us trick-or-treating? Yes!" squealed Justine.

I was about to say, "What happened to handing out candy?" but I was getting a little better at thinking before I said anything. And in that one teensy moment I realized something: Lexie had made a costume, and now she was offering to take Justine and me out. That could only mean one thing: She wanted to go trick-or-treating herself after all. She just didn't want to admit it.

"Yes," I said cautiously. "That would be great. Thanks, Lexie. But what about Daddy Bo? He thinks he's taking us."

"I'll talk to him," said my sister, and she shouldered her violin case and headed down Twelfth Street like a steamship leaving harbor.

Twenty minutes later it was all arranged. Daddy Bo would help Mom and Dad hand out the candy, and Lexie, dressed as Dorothy from *The Wizard of Oz*, would take Justine and me trick-or-treating.

12

Early on Halloween morning our doorbell rang. I answered it, eating a piece of toast, and there stood a fairy princess.

"Happy Halloween! May all your dreams come true," said the princess, waving her wand around in the air and throwing something sparkly and pink onto the rug in our front hallway.

It was Justine, and she was very excited. She bounced up and down 4x.

My mother came into the hall and saw the sparkly stuff. She eyed the closet where we keep our vacuum cleaner, but she didn't say anything except, "Good morning, Justine."

"Good morning! Good morning! We're having a party

in our classroom this afternoon!" Justine was bouncing again. "Pearl, why aren't you wearing your costume?"

I remembered that the first graders get to wear their costumes all day long. Fourth graders don't, though. I pointed to a shopping bag. "It's in there," I told her. "We're supposed to put our costumes on after lunch. Mom, you're going to come to the parade, aren't you? And our party? Daddy Bo too?" (I already knew that Dad wouldn't be able to come, but he had come the year before when I was a skunk, so that was all right.)

"We'll be there," said Mom, and she sounded excited. Halloween does that to you.

The day was a great big whirl of costumes and excitement and treats, plus the costume parade in the gym. Daddy Bo was the only grandparent who came to my class party, and everyone was glad to see him. Halfway through our parade he quietly attached a fake squirrel tail to the back of his pants. One by one my classmates noticed it and started laughing. Even Rachel and Katie and Jill laughed. Even Jill's *mother* laughed. (I was steering clear of Jill's mother due to the incident with the police, but Mrs. DiNunzio didn't seem to have a problem with me, and she even smiled at me once, and later talked to my mother and Daddy Bo.) The point is that everyone thought the squirrel tail was funny and wanted to say so to Daddy Bo. From inside his molar costume, James Brubaker the Third said, "That is hilarious,

Mr. . . ." He turned to me and whispered, "What's his name?"

"Daddy Bo," I whispered back.

"That is hilarious, Mr. Bo." He stuck his arm out of the tooth and shook Daddy Bo's hand.

On the way home from school, walking in a group with Mom, Daddy Bo, Mr. and Mrs. Lebarro, and Justine (who had used up all her fairy dust), I glanced up and down Sixth Avenue and said, "It's almost time."

"Almost time for what?" asked Daddy Bo.

Justine looked at Daddy Bo like he was a sadly uninformed kindergartener. "Time for the parade!" she exclaimed.

"Another parade?"

"The big parade through the Village, Dad," said my mother. (She calls him Dad even though he's my father's father. She calls her own father Dad too, which is probably confusing for both grandfathers.)

"Even grown-ups walk in this parade," said Justine.

"The costumes are elaborate," spoke up Mr. Lebarro.

"My, what a day," said Daddy Bo.

It certainly was. Daddy Bo and Lexie and I watched a teensy bit of the parade from the end of our street later, but then we hurried home for trick-or-treating.

Daddy Bo helped me assemble my costume: the scarves, the stockings, the eye patch, the flag, my beard, a bag for which I had made a tag that read PIECES OF

ATE, and of course the hook hand. Daddy Bo speared the treasure map with the hook so that the map would dangle from it as I walked along.

"Wow, Pearl!" cried Lexie when she entered the family room as Dorothy Gale. "You look great!"

I was a little surprised at how detailed Lexie's costume was. I had thought that maybe she would just find a blue-and-white-checked dress and a pair of red shoes. And she had, but she was also wearing thin blue socks and had tied a blue ribbon in her hair and was carrying a basket with a little stuffed Toto dog peeking out of it. Way more surprising was that her other hand was carrying a plastic pumpkin. As in for collecting candy. So I was right. Lexie wanted to go trick-or-treating after all. I was about to point this out, but then I reminded myself about the list of rules, which I felt had prevented four to six fights already, so all I said was, "You look great too."

When Lexie smiled hugely at me I thought that maybe I should add an eleventh rule to my list. It would be: Compliment her once in a while.

It was time to go. Lexie and I posed in the family room while Mom took pictures of us in our costumes, and then we headed for Justine's apartment. We left Daddy Bo behind, still wearing the squirrel tail and happily handing out candy every time our doorbell rang.

"Hi! Hi!" shrieked Justine when she saw us. "I'm all ready!"

"Honey, you need to calm down just a little bit," her mother said to her.

Why? I wondered. It was Halloween, for heaven's sake.

"Let's start on the top floor and work our way down to the lobby," suggested Lexie. "We'll take the stairs so we don't have to wait for the elevator."

So we trudged up to the twelfth floor, meeting a few other trick-or-treaters (a mouse, a cactus, Miss Piggy) on the way.

"I call ringing the doorbells!" shouted Justine as she burst through the SERVICE door and into the twelfth-floor hallway. "All the doorbells!" She ran to the nearest one, punched the bell 3x, and yelled, "Trick or treat! Trick or treat!"

Maybe she did need to calm down.

The door opened, apparently by itself, and when we peered inside we saw a big dark space lit by orange candles. Suddenly a skeleton's hand holding three candy bars reached out from behind the door. Justine shrieked, only this time she was scared, not excited. She tried to hide behind Lexie. The hand, which was attached to someone very tall wearing a Grim Reaper costume, dropped a Butterfinger bar into each of our pumpkins. Then we heard creepy laughter and the door closed slowly.

Justine was quieter after that. But by the time we reached the tenth floor and no other scary things had happened she started smiling again. She was about to ring Mrs. Mott's bell when suddenly I began barking. Lexie turned to me in horror.

"Pearl! What are you—"

"I don't want any treats from Mrs. Mott," I whispered loudly. "I want to trick her!"

"Well, come on then," said Lexie. She pulled Justine and me into the stairwell and closed the door behind us just as Mrs. Mott's door banged open and we heard her call, "There's that dog again, Hal!"

Lexie laughed so hard that she dropped her pumpkin and all her candy scattered out. I couldn't help noticing that she had just as much candy as Justine and I did. (But I didn't say anything.)

We continued on our way toward the lobby, one floor at a time, our buckets—all three of them—growing heavier, and when we stepped into the fourth-floor hallway, I heard Lexie draw in her breath. "Uh-oh," she said softly.

"What—," I started to say, but I stopped talking when I saw a girl Lexie's age at the other end of the hall. I recognized Mandy Stanworth, one of Lexie's classmates, not to mention a person who doesn't live in our apartment building. What I am trying to say is that Lexie didn't expect to run into Mandy or anyone else she knows.

116

Mandy was walking with two little kids, holding tight to their hands. The kids were dressed as a cat and a dog, and they were carrying orange treat bags that said BOO on each side. Mandy, I hate to point out, was not wearing a costume—or carrying a bag.

"Lexie!" exclaimed Mandy, and she began to laugh. "What are you *doing*?"

Well, by now it was plain to just about everyone in the world, probably even babies, that my sister was trick-or-treating. It was also plain that Mandy Stanworth was not trick-or-treating.

"She's—," said Justine, but I clapped my hand over her mouth.

Lexie's face had turned as red as the skull eyes on my flag. She took a step backward. I let go of Justine's mouth. "My sister's taking my friend Justine and me trick-or-treating," I spoke up. "That's Justine," I added, pointing to her. "And I'm Pearl Littlefield, Lexie's sister. By the way, in case you couldn't tell, I'm a pirate and Justine's a fairy godmother."

"Fairy *princess*!" said Justine fiercely.

"Lexie didn't want to wear a costume," I went on, "but I had a tantrum and I yelled, 'I can't go trick-or-treating unless my sister goes with me! And she has to wear a costume!' I screamed and cried until my parents made her dress up like Dorothy."

Here, Mandy shot Lexie a look of sympathy mixed with exasperation about little sisters. She even clucked her tongue like an old person.

"Hey, Lexie," I continued, inspired. "Make sure you don't lose that bucket of candy for Sally."

"Who's Sally?" asked Justine, but luckily her mouth was full of M&M's and I was the only one who understood what she had said.

Lexie laughed shakily. "Yeah. For Sally." She hesitated, glancing at me.

I glared at my sister. Did I have to do *all* the work? "Sally is our cousin," I informed Mandy. (We actually have zero cousins.) "She came down with the flu today so Lexie said, 'Well, as long as I have to take Pearl and Justine trick-or-treating I might as well collect candy for Sally. That way her Halloween won't be a total loss.'"

Mandy nodded wisely, as if on some other Halloween she had had to collect candy for a cousin with the flu.

"Can we go?" asked Justine, stuffing her hand into her bucket again and pulling out a chocolate pumpkin. She began to unpeel the wrapper.

Lexie placed her own hand gently over Justine's. "Justine, honey, you're going to make yourself sick. You know your mother told you not to eat any candy before you get home."

Mrs. Lebarro had said no such thing, but I saw that

Lexie had a good idea. I reached into my bucket. "Lexie? Can I eat a Hershey bar? Please?"

"Oh, Pearl, honey, no, no, no!"

"Let's *go*!" squawked Justine. "I want to *go*!"

It certainly looked like Lexie had her hands full with us. She shook her head ruefully at Mandy, and Mandy rolled her eyes and whispered, "Good luck," before stepping onto the elevator.

Justine and Lexie and I stood in a row in the hallway until the doors had closed. As soon as we could see that the elevator had reached the third floor, Lexie squeezed my hand. "Thanks," she said.

"You're welcome."

I hope I don't sound conceited when I say that I was very proud of myself.

13

We didn't run into Mandy again, but I knew Lexie was worried that we would because she kept peering around corners and through doorways like she was in a spy movie.

"What are you doing?" Justine asked her.

And Lexie was all, "Oh, nothing, nothing." But she definitely didn't want to get caught again.

Luckily, the third floor was empty, and on the second floor we ran into a dad with three very tiny trick-or-treaters, but that was it. No Mandy. No one else Lexie knew. At least no one her age. When we rang the bell of #2A, which was the last apartment in the entire building, the door was opened by Mr. Berman, who plays the saxophone in big orchestras and who Lexie thinks is handsome, even though he's thirty-one and has a mole on his eyelid.

"Hello, girls," said Mr. Berman, dropping Chunky bars into our buckets. "Happy Halloween!"

"Thank you," said Lexie. "I'm just taking Pearl and Justine around. You know. Babysitting and whatever. Have you played in any Broadway shows recently?"

Mr. Berman and Lexie stood there chatting for so long that Justine plopped onto the hallway floor. She looked like she was ready to dump her bucket out and start sorting candy, so I said, "Lexie, is it all right if Justine and I go down to the lobby to show John our costumes? We'll wait for you there."

"Okay," replied Lexie, and then immediately forgot about us. I know this because right away she said, "Mr. Berman, how often do Broadway orchestras need new violin players?"

"Come on," I said to Justine and led her into the stairwell again. We marched down the stairs. At the bottom were two doors. I pushed the nearest one open and we ran through it and the door slammed shut behind us and suddenly we were standing all in shadows, like if we were in the woods at nighttime, which I have never been, but I can imagine it.

"Hey, why is it dark?" yelped Justine. I could barely see her.

"I think we went through the wrong door," I said.

I took off my hook hand, felt behind me for the handle, and turned it.

Nothing happened.

I rattled it.

"Open the door!" wailed Justine

"I'm trying to!" I twisted the handle again and rattled it some more and then I banged it with my fist.

Nothing.

"It's locked," I told her, rubbing my hand. "Ow."

"But where's John?"

"Through the other door. In the lobby. I think this is the door to the basement."

"The basement? I hate the basement! Get us out of here, Pearl!"

I felt around for a light switch, hoping I wouldn't find a spider instead. I didn't. But I didn't find a switch either.

"Pearl!" yowled Justine, starting to cry.

I pounded on the door. "Help!" I shouted. *Bam, bam, bam.* "Help!"

Justine dropped her bucket (I could hear candy scatter), and she banged and yelled too.

"Help! Somebody help us!" I shrieked.

"We're trapped in the dungeon!" shouted Justine. "Help! Help! I don't want to die here!"

I felt around for a light switch again, and this time I found one. I flicked it up and in the dim glow I saw that we were at the top of a flight of stairs, the creepy stairs down to the basement. There was a window in the door, but not the kind you can really see through. It was thick, and sandwiched in the middle of it was chicken wire. I stood on my tiptoes and tried to see through the window anyway.

"Hello?" I called. "Hello?"

"HEEEEEEELP!" yelled Justine.

"Justine, be quiet for a minute." I slid down until I was sitting on the floor, my back to the door.

"*What are you doing?*" (Justine was saying everything at top volume, and like it was followed by a whole lot of !!!!!!s.)

"I'm thinking. Just let me think."

Justine was quiet for about one and a half seconds. Then she whammed the door with her foot.

"Stop it," I said. "You're going to hurt yourself." I stood up. "Okay. I will rescue us."

"How?" asked Justine suspiciously.

I had no idea. But I crept down the stairs to see what I could find.

Justine stood silently above, watching.

At the bottom I turned a corner. All around me were dim shapes that I couldn't quite make out. Boxes, I thought, and maybe old furniture covered with sheets. And some cans of paint. I stared at the cans, and then suddenly I grabbed one.

From the top of the steps I heard a faint scratching

123

noise, which turned out to be Justine gathering her candy back into her bucket. She glanced at me as I hurried up the stairs again.

"What's that for?" she asked.

"Watch." I aimed the bucket at the window, but before I could heave it I said, "Wait. Go sit down there."

"Into the *base*ment?"

"Just go down about five steps, out of the way."

"No."

"If you don't move I can't break the window and we'll be stuck here forever in the dungeon."

Justine clattered down the stairs.

And I bashed the can of paint into the glass. Some of it cracked and chipped away, but most of it was held in place by the chicken wire. I swung the can again. *Crash*.

"Pearl? Justine?"

At the sound of the voice I lost my balance, dropped the can, and fell on the floor.

"Pearl?" called the voice again. It belonged to a man and it was coming from the other side of the door.

"Yes! Yes! It's me!"

"And me, Justine Lebarro!" shouted Justine, scrambling back up the stairs.

"I'm going to open the door now." I recognized John's voice. "But put down whatever you were using to break the window."

"I already did," I replied. I stepped aside and the door swung open.

"Are you okay?" Lexie was hovering behind John.

"We're okay," I said.

"No, we're not. We were trapped in the dungeon!" exclaimed Justine.

Lexie sounded a little bit like maybe she wanted to laugh, but then she got a good look at the shattered window. "Pearl, what were you *do*ing?"

"Getting us out of here, duh."

"But what were you going to do after you broke the window?"

"Yell through it," I said.

"Okay. Because I certainly hope you weren't going to try to crawl through it. See how sharp the glass is?"

"I know how sharp glass is," I said crossly. "And anyway, a person can't crawl through chicken wire."

John was twisting the knob thoughtfully. "We need to put a sign on this door," he announced.

Justine looked interested. "One that says THIS WAY TO THE DUNGEON?"

"I was thinking of DO NOT ENTER."

"You need to be more specific," I told him. "The sign should say CAUTION: DOOR LOCKS BEHIND YOU."

John looked impressed. "That's a good idea, Pearl."

"Thank you," I said. Then I added, "I'm sorry I broke the window."

"Don't worry, John," spoke up Lexie, using her most annoying adult voice. "My parents will talk to the building manager about the incident. We'll pay to have the window fixed."

By the time John had accompanied Lexie and Justine and me to the seventh floor and explained to our parents what had happened, and all the adults had looked us over and seen for themselves that we weren't injured, I was starting to feel better.

"Pearl saved the day," Justine declared.

"Well, really John did," I said modestly.

"But Pearl was going to rescue us. She had a plan. Also, I cried, but Pearl didn't. She remained calm, like in a fire drill."

"I thought I heard you yelling, Pearl," said Lexie.

I narrowed my eyes at her. "If I hadn't yelled, how would you have known where to find us?"

"A very good point," spoke up Daddy Bo.

Mom said, "Well, it's been quite a night. I think it's time for everyone to go to bed." By "everyone" she meant Lexie and Justine and me.

So the Lebarros went back to their apartment and Lexie and I climbed into the bunk beds. Bitey settled himself on my chest.

"Pearl?" said Lexie even though she had already turned out the light and usually didn't like to talk after that point. "Why did you panic tonight? I know you panicked too. It wasn't only Justine."

"Because we were trapped in the basement!" I almost added "duh" again. "Without any food!"

"Without any food? You guys had two buckets of candy with you."

"You know I don't like candy." The only thing I like that's sweet is gum.

Lexie sighed. She might have groaned a little too. "So *why* do you go trick-or-treating every year?"

"Because I like to dress up. And for the fun of sorting the candy," I told her. "I like to see how much I got before I give it away." (I always take my candy to the hospital on Eighth Avenue so that kids who can't go out on Halloween can at least have some treats.)

There was silence from the upper bunk and I thought Lexie might have fallen asleep, but then her voice floated crabbily down to me. "Well, what kind of kid doesn't like candy?"

I stroked Bitey's head. "One who doesn't have any cavities," I replied, and realized I could add something positive to my comparison chart the next day:

	☹ Lexie	☺ Pearl
Cavities	4	0

There was another little silence and then I said, "Hey, did you know that because my teeth are perfect I get extra money from the Tooth Fairy?"

Lexie is far too old to get Tooth Fairy money anymore. Even so, she leaned over the side of the bed and peered at me. "What? How much do you get?"

"Five bucks per tooth."

"Five bucks?! The most I ever got was a dollar fifty."

That was the most I'd ever gotten too, but this was fun. "Perfect teeth mean a lot to the Tooth Fairy," I said.

"Aw, man." Lexie heaved herself back onto her bed and flopped down so hard that above me her mattress shook.

I smiled to myself in the darkness.

Daddy Bo and I developed a routine. Every day after I came home from school we would sit in the kitchen together and have a snack. Daddy Bo would eat our leftover Halloween candy (Almond Joy bars), and I would eat apple slices with peanut butter.

"Ah, this is the life," said Daddy Bo on the Thursday after Halloween. He bit into an Almond Joy. Then he turned around, pulled open the drawer where the candy was kept, peered into it, and said sadly, "Only four bars left."

"We'll get some more," I told him, although I wasn't sure that was the best idea, considering what I knew about old people and dentures.

The apartment was very quiet. Dad was at work, Lexie was out with Dallas (I think they were on a *date*), and Mom had closed herself into her closet-office.

Bitey wandered into the kitchen, jumped two feet straight into the air as if he had seen Dr. Pritchard (Dr. Pritchard is his vet), and ran out.

We ignored him.

"Well," said Daddy Bo, crumpling his candy wrapper, "I guess you have homework to do, don't you?"

"Um . . . yes."

I did have homework. We were supposed to write a composition about bugs, but I was not inspired by the assignment. I don't like bugs.

"Okay." Daddy Bo sighed.

"What are you going to do?" I asked. Daddy Bo seemed to be at loose ends. I am often in the same boat.

Another sigh. "Watch the Weather Channel, I suppose."

I don't like the Weather Channel except for the shots of tidal waves, which their scientific name is tsunamis. "All right," I replied. "I'll see you in a little while."

I heaved an enormous, annoyed sigh, sat at Lexie's desk, and stared at a sheet of lined paper. Finally I wrote, "I don't like bugs."

I set the composition aside, found my pad of drawing paper, and worked busily on a picture of a tsunami rolling out of the elevator and onto the tenth floor just as Mrs. Mott opened her door. I was making a cartoon bubble over Mrs. Mott's head that said, "Oh, no! A tsunami has arrived in New York City!" when suddenly I realized how quiet the apartment was. I stood up and listened. No television sounds.

"Daddy Bo?" I called.

I walked down the hall to the family room. It was empty. The TV was turned off. That was when I saw that the door to our apartment was open.

Uh-oh.

I closed the door, then looked all around until I saw Bitey. "Good boy," I said to him. "I'm glad you didn't escape."

I was wondering what to do next when the apartment phone rang, the one that's connected to the lobby and the garage. I made a dash for it, picked it up, and said breathlessly, "Hello? John?"

"Hi, Pearl. Is your mother there?"

Out of long habit I answered, "Yes-but-she-can't-come-to-the-phone-right-now."

"Well"—John cleared his throat—"your grandfather's down here and, um, I think someone might want to come and get him."

A funny feeling crept into my stomach. "Okay," I said. "Let me—"

Before I could finish my sentence, John added, "You might want to bring his shoes."

Bring Daddy Bo's shoes? The funny feeling grew stronger.

"Okay," I said again, and hung up.

I ran to Mom's door and was about to knock on it when I heard her phone ring. "What do you mean the galleys are lost?" she cried a moment later.

I didn't know what she was talking about, but I did not like her tone of voice. I hurried into my old room and saw Daddy Bo's sneakers by the bed. I grabbed them, ran to the kitchen, then grabbed the key to our apartment and let myself into the hall. I punched the elevator button 9x, as if that would actually make it come faster.

When it did arrive, Mrs. Mott was on it. I considered barking at her, but decided to keep her in the dark a little while longer. It was much more fun if she thought that some dog kept getting loose on the tenth floor.

"Pearl Littlefield, whose shoes are those?" asked Mrs. Mott with her squinty eyes fastened on the sneakers. I don't know why Mrs. Mott always calls kids by both of their names.

"They're my grandfather's, Sheila Mott," I replied.

Mrs. Mott shrugged up her shoulders. I was sure she had more questions for me, but my rudeness had quieted her. As the elevator doors were opening, though, she said, "Just remember who you're talking to." (I could see that her lips were ready to add "Pearl Littlefield" to the end of her sentence, but she thought better of it.)

"Whom," I told her. "It's 'Just remember *whom* you're talking to.'" I actually wasn't sure if "whom" was correct, but sometimes it is.

"Watch your tongue," was all Mrs. Mott could think to say.

She stepped into the lobby and we saw Daddy Bo sitting on the red couch next to John's doorman station. Daddy Bo was chatting away about the Mets, and John was smiling and nodding—the way you smile and nod when a person you don't know at all says hello to you, or when someone is talking to you and doesn't realize he has toilet paper trailing out of his pants. Or when, as in the case of Daddy Bo, the person is wearing a suit and tie—and is barefoot. Daddy Bo's legs were crossed, and he was vigorously massaging the toes of his right foot with both hands.

I ran ahead of Mrs. Mott and reached Daddy Bo first.

"Pearl!" he exclaimed. "There you are!" Like we hadn't just eaten our snacks together.

I shot a look at John, then jabbed my thumb in the direction of Mrs. Mott, who had stopped to inspect the cleanliness of the mailroom, and had just turned on the light with the tip of her cane.

John nodded at me and disappeared into the mailroom. I could hear him say, "Good afternoon, Mrs. Mott," in a courtly manner, like she was the queen, which I'm sure she thought she was.

"John, the mailroom is a disgrace," replied Mrs. Mott. (It was as neat as a pin.)

John took her by the elbow and steered her the long way around Daddy Bo and out the front door saying, "I'll get right on it," and, "Let me call a cab for you."

By the time he returned I had helped Daddy Bo put his shoes on. "John, about the mail," said Daddy Bo in a cheerful tone. "I was wondering why it isn't here yet. It seems to me that it's been coming later and later every day."

A pained expression crossed John's face. "Well, sir," he said, and I realized I had never heard him call Mrs. Mott "ma'am." "Sir," he said again, "actually, well, actually, it already came today. Remember? You picked it up just before Lexie dropped Pearl and Justine off."

It was true. Our mail was sitting on the kitchen counter.

Daddy Bo looked momentarily troubled. Then he said, "To quote Pirate Pearl, blimey!"

(I don't think I have ever said "blimey," but it did sound like a good pirate expression.)

"Daddy Bo, come on. Let's go back upstairs." I held out my hand to him. "Maybe you can help me with my homework. I have to write about bugs, and I don't know what to say."

"Bugs," repeated Daddy Bo. "Huh. I'm not sure how much I know about them."

We started for the elevator. While we were waiting for it I turned around and mouthed "Thanks" to John, who gave me the thumbs-up sign.

The elevator was passing the second floor when Daddy Bo looked down and noticed that he was wearing his suit and his sneakers and no socks. "Uh-oh," he said.

We were standing side by side, holding hands. "I know," I replied.

Daddy Bo pointed to his feet. "How did—?" he started to ask. "Where are—? Pearl, perhaps this little adventure should be our secret. Just between you and me."

"Really?" This seemed like one of those things I should probably mention to Mom and Dad. But Daddy Bo was looking at me pleadingly, the way Bitey had looked at me the day he'd found a cockroach in the bathroom and really wanted to play with it. "All right," I said at last.

We let ourselves back into the apartment. Mom was still closed into her office and still yelling into the phone. I returned the key to the kitchen. Then I found a pair of Daddy Bo's socks and together we removed his sneakers, got the socks on, and replaced the sneakers with slippers.

"Blimey," said Daddy Bo, looking very pleased with his feet.

After dinner that night I asked Lexie if I could have the bedroom to myself for a little while and she said yes because she had to practice her violin anyway. I sat at the desk, looked at the bug composition, to which I had added, with Daddy Bo's help, "They bite and sting and some of them smell." Daddy Bo had said it was important to back up your opinions. Then he had said, "Are you sure you don't want to include some more details?" So I had written another sentence. "By the way, cockroaches can run really fast." I knew this because Bitey's had gotten away from him. "It's a detail *and* an interesting fact," I said to Daddy Bo.

I stuck the composition in my notebook so I wouldn't lose it before I got to school the next day. Then I ripped a blank piece of paper out of the notebook and wrote:

Daddy Bo's List Of Things To Wear
(Or Bring) When Leaving The Apartment

1. Shirt
2. Pants (extremly important)
3. Belt
4. Socks
5. Shoes
6. Underwear (well no one will know if you don't have it)
7. Jacket if it is cold outside
8. Wallet
9. Key to the apartment
10. Pearl's map of the building if necesary

"Daddy Bo?" I called, sticking my head into the hall-way.

"In here," he replied. His voice floated to me from my old room.

Daddy Bo was sitting on the bed and his feet were bare again. I hoped this wasn't going to become a habit because frankly his toenails could use some work.

I handed him the paper. "This is for you," I said. "I was thinking about what happened today, and I thought a list might be helpful."

Daddy Bo took the paper and scanned it. "What can I say? You're a gem, Pearl. I'll keep this handy and consult it every day."

"Really?"

"Really. Thank you for being so thoughtful."

"You're welcome." I climbed into Daddy Bo's lap and patted his chin. "What's this for?" I asked him.

Daddy Bo looked uncertain. "What's it for? It's my chin. Sorry it's so floppy."

"That's okay."

I tried to make myself laugh by picturing Mrs. Mott and the tenth-floor tsunami, but it didn't work.

15

One Sunday afternoon I laid my pirate costume out on the floor of Lexie's room and studied it. I wanted to be able to change it into a spy costume. I considered the hook hand and the flag and the pieces of eight and the medallion. What did a spy need? I wondered. I thought for a moment. It sort of depended on how modern the spy was. New spies needed computers and video cameras and speedy cars. Old-fashioned spies were less complicated. They pretty much only needed a magnifying glass, a fingerprinting kit, and a good disguise. Sadly, I didn't have any of these things. Not even the good disguise, because the thing that makes a disguise good is if you can blend into a crowd when you're wearing it, and one thing I could not do dressed as a pirate was blend into a crowd.

My whole costume was useless, spy-wise.

"Too bad, Bitey," I said. Bitey was curled up in the exact center of my pillow. He opened one eye, licked his front paw, and went back to sleep. He wasn't the tiniest bit interested in my problem.

My problem was that I wanted to spy on Lexie and Dallas, but I didn't have a spy costume. My big sister and her boyfriend were in the family room doing something, and Mom and Dad had said they were not to be disturbed. So Daddy Bo was taking a nap in his room, and Mom and Dad were catching up on chores, and I was supposed to be finishing my weekend homework, but how could I concentrate on Japan and amphibians when Lexie and Dallas might be kissing in the family room?

I really, really needed a periscope.

Finally I remembered something I had learned on TV: The best way to hide is in plain sight. In other words, not to hide at all. So I casually stepped out of the bedroom, not even bothering to be quiet. I walked down the hall, humming, like I was just on my way to the kitchen for a juice box.

"Hum-de-hum-de-hum." I paused outside the family room and took a good look in there, and in that instance I realized why not many grown-ups choose spying as a career. All Lexie and Dallas were doing was sitting next to each other at the table with their school

139

books open in front of them and the computer on, clearly working on some kind of project.

"We have to list ten sources," Lexie was saying to Dallas.

Well. This couldn't have been more of a disappointment.

"Pearl?" I heard my father call from the bedroom.

"Yeah?" I grabbed a juice box.

"Can you come here for a minute, please?"

I found Mom and Dad in their room. The vacuum cleaner was sitting by the door and their bed was covered with piles of clean laundry.

"Do you need some help?" I asked, in case Dad was going to say anything about spies or spying.

"What a nice offer," he replied. "Yes. I was just about to ask if you could fold these things and put them away." He pointed to several of the piles on the bed. "The towels go in the linen closet, and the clothes belong to you and Lexie."

I carried the piles to our room. I tossed Lexie's pile up onto the top bunk. Then I folded my clothes and jammed them into the dresser. I was opening the door to the linen closet a few minutes later when I heard a shriek from the family room. No one in my family shrieks like that except Lexie. And it was not a happy shriek. It was the kind of sound Lexie would make if she had found a snake in the apartment. Actually, it was the kind of sound she would make if I had embarrassed her by wandering around in my underwear and frog slippers in front of Dallas. But I had my list of rules now so there was no chance of that happening.

The door to my parents' room was closed, and this seemed like another emergency, so I didn't bother to ask permission to interrupt Lexie and Dallas. I dropped the towels and ran into the family room. This is what I saw:

- Dallas was sitting at the table. He was staring at Lexie. His mouth was open a little bit.
- Lexie was on her feet in the middle of the room. A deep blush was creeping across her face. She was approx. the color of the plum I had found when I was cleaning out my old bedroom.

At first I thought Dallas had tried to kiss my sister. I know I would look wild and red-faced if a boy tried to kiss me. But then I noticed one other thing in the room:

- Bitey. He was running in circles, and trailing from his mouth was a bra.

Right away I realized it was Lexie's bra, because it was smaller than my mother's bras, and also because it had a pink-and-yellow rose in the center between the two pointy parts. As I watched, fascinated, Bitey flung the bra in the air, pounced on it when it landed, and pulled the rose off. Then he flung the rose in the air, as if he'd caught a pink-and-yellow baby mouse.

Lexie shrieked again, and now Dallas's face turned red.

I was wondering what would happen next when Lexie noticed me and yanked me down the hall and into our room. She slammed the door shut behind us and looked all around the room, including on the top bunk. Then she said fiercely, "Did Mom and Dad ask you to put the laundry away?"

I nodded.

"Well, can't you do anything right?"

"Me? What did I do wrong?" I put my hands on my hips. I was about to tell my sister that, once again, she reminded me quite a bit of Mrs. Mott, but then I remembered items #7, #8, and #9 on my list of rules.

I took a deep breath and kept my mouth shut.

"Dallas saw my bra!" wailed Lexie.

"I know. That was awful," I said, with honest sympathy. "But it wasn't exactly my fault."

"Are you kidding me?" Lexie inclined her head toward her bed, where the laundry I had tossed up there was now spilling over the side. It was clear that Bitey had been playing in it. "Pearl, you are so lazy. If you had actually bothered to put the laundry *away,* then Bitey wouldn't have gotten my bra."

"Well, I didn't know he was going to drag it into the living room! He thought that up all by himself."

"Because you left my stuff out in the open."

"I was *going* to fold it," I said.

Lexie muttered something about a road and good intentions and also said a four-letter word that I am not allowed to use. Then she raised her voice. "But you didn't fold it. Or put it away. You left it out and Bitey got my bra and now Dallas has *seen* it."

I pulled a piece of gum from a pack lying on the desk, and stuck it in my mouth. "You know, this is not really such a big problem. Why can't you just pretend the bra is Mom's? Dallas doesn't know anything about bras. He's a boy."

"He still saw a bra," Lexie snapped.

I considered the situation. "Okay," I said at last. "I know what to do."

I marched back to the family room. Lexie followed me suspiciously. "Can you believe it?" I said to Dallas, who hadn't moved an inch since we'd left him. He looked sort of like John had looked when Daddy Bo was sitting in the lobby in his bare feet, not remembering that the mail had already arrived.

"Um . . . ," said Dallas.

"Bitey got Mom's underwear!" I was careful not to use the word "bra," since I didn't think it would be safe for my sister's face to get any more red than it already was.

I didn't look at Lexie or Dallas—or Bitey, who was now asleep under the table. I just snatched up the bra and the rose and hurried back to our bedroom.

I closed the door behind me. But one second later it opened and in walked Lexie.

"What happened to knocking?" I asked her.

Lexie glared at me. "Don't think this is over, Pearl," she said. "I have to go back out there because I can't leave Dallas sitting around thinking about bras. But this is the worst thing you have ever done to me and I do not forgive you."

She turned smartly, like a soldier, and left the room.

I sat at the desk and frowned into space. This seemed a little unreasonable, even for Lexie. Okay, so I had left the laundry on her bed. But it wasn't like I had found her bra, stuck it in Bitey's mouth, and shoved him into the family room.

This was puzzling. I pulled out my list of rules and studied it. Items #5 and #6 caught my attention: Don't show Lexie's boyfriend her baby blanket, and Don't talk about her throw-up. They seemed related to the bra problem, but I wasn't sure how. I thought about Lexie's reaction to the baby blanket, the throw-up incident, and now the bra. I felt like I was taking a test at school: Explain why these three things belong together. And at last the answer came to me: It was the whole embarrassment thing again. Lexie was very, very embarrassed. I didn't know why she got so embarrassed about some things, but she did, and when she was embarrassed she got mad. Usually at me.

I stood up from the desk and held the bra for a while, turning it around in my hands. Out of curiosity, I considered trying it on over my T-shirt, but then I imagined my sister catching me, so that was the end of that idea. At last I folded Lexie's clothes, including the ruined bra, and placed them neatly in the bureau.

At dinner that night Dad said, "So, Lexie, did you and Dallas get a lot of work done on your project?"

Lexie glanced at me, and in my head I scrolled down the list of rules again. Number 3 came to mind. So did #8. And of course #5 and #6. I desperately wanted to tell Mom and Dad and Daddy Bo about Bitey and the flying bra. Instead I just looked at Lexie with great interest, like I couldn't wait to hear about the project and whether she and Dallas had found ten sources. I was not about to say anything else that would embarrass her.

"We're almost done," Lexie said finally, in sort of a small voice. "We can finish in school tomorrow."

After dinner, while Lexie was practicing her violin in the family room, I sat at the desk and wrote a note.

> Dear Lexie,
>   I am deeply sorry I stole your bra and showed it to Dallas. It was thoughtless and I will not do that again.
>   Love, Bitey 🐷

I put the note under my sister's pillow. She found it when we were going to bed. I had expected her to laugh, or at least to give me a tiny, fake smile, but she didn't do either one. She just crumpled the note and tossed it into the wastebasket. "Like I said," she told me, "this isn't over."

It was the maddest I had ever seen Lexie.

16

On Thanksgiving morning, Daddy Bo said to me, "What time am I going home today?"

Daddy Bo and I were having breakfast in the family room. We'd been given permission to eat on the couch instead of at the table, because the Macy's Thanksgiving parade was almost on and we wanted to watch it in comfort.

I balanced my plate on my knees. I was determined not to spill a crumb, since I hoped to be able to eat on the couch again in the near future.

"What?" I replied.

"When am I going home?" asked Daddy Bo.

I wasn't sure how to answer the question. Finally I said carefully, "Justine and her parents are coming over at four o'clock."

"But what about me?"

"You're already here."

"I thought I was going home for Thanksgiving. I'm always at home on holidays."

I didn't point out that he hadn't been home at Halloween. Instead I said, "Don't you want to have Thanksgiving here with us? We're going to have lots of fun at dinner. We got poppers with prizes and paper hats inside, and Justine always makes everyone wear the hats until dinner is over."

"Poppers? What poppers?" Daddy Bo was sounding somewhat grouchy.

"*Pop*pers. Dad said you used to have poppers when he was growing up. At Thanksgiving and at Christmas too. It's because of your poppers that we have poppers now."

Daddy Bo grunted and picked up the remote.

"Don't change the channel!" I yelped. "The parade is going to begin in four minutes."

"What parade?"

"The Thanks*giv*ing parade. That's why we're eating on the couch."

Daddy Bo looked mystified. I took the remote away from him.

The parade started. The Snoopy balloon went by, and then a giant rainbow-colored turkey on a float, and then Daddy Bo said, "So what time am I going home today?"

I thought about my rules for living with Lexie and applied #9 to Daddy Bo. "We're eating here," I told him again. "The Lebarros are coming over. Remember? Poppers?" I felt an eye roll coming on, but I know how annoying it is when Lexie rolls her eyes.

At the first commercial, I took our empty plates into the kitchen where Mom and Dad were fussing with cookbooks and bowls of food. (Lexie was still asleep, by the way. When she became a teenager she suddenly needed a bra, a boyfriend, and lots of sleep.)

"I'm going to start the place cards now," I announced. That was the Thanksgiving job I had volunteered for: making place cards for the dinner table.

I was about to add that Daddy Bo wanted to go home for Thanksgiving, but just then Mom spilled a can of cling peaches across the counter and the syrupy juice dripped down onto the floor and she said in a very high-pitched voice, "Pearl, get Bitey out of here while I clean this up! It's sticky!" She really is better at writing than cooking, and Thanksgiving makes her nervous.

I scooped up Bitey, plunked him on the couch next to Daddy Bo, and gathered my art supplies. I spread them out on the table and worked on the place cards during commercials. The cards looked like this:

I was very proud of them. Even Lexie probably couldn't make pop-up, 3-D cards.

I had finished three when Lexie, yawning, finally staggered into the family room. "Let's get dressed and go to the parade," she said. "It seems silly to watch it on TV when we could see it for real." I was surprised that Lexie was speaking to me, since she had barely even looked at me since the Day of the Bra. Maybe the holiday had softened her up.

"Mom and Dad won't let us go by ourselves," I replied.

"Hello. We'll go with Daddy Bo."

I considered this. "Um, I'm not so sure."

Lexie glanced at Daddy Bo, who had gotten the remote again, and who was clutching it while he frowned at a bunch of dancing elves on a float. "I'm going to ask Mom and Dad anyway," she said.

To my surprise, Mom seemed thrilled to get rid of us for a while, and she threw Dad out of the apartment too. "Go. Go have fun," she said. She opened another cookbook, yanked a bag of flour out of a cupboard, and closed the refrigerator door with her foot.

So the four of us took the subway uptown and waded through the swarms of people who were trying to get a glimpse of the parade. Despite all the noise and confusion Daddy Bo's mood improved almost instantly. When we caught sight of the top of the Clifford balloon, Daddy Bo suddenly shouted, "Go, dog, go!" which was a little strange, but whatever.

A few moments later, Lexie called, "Here! Over here!"

She had found a hole in the crowd, and we all slithered into it and got a good view of the parade just as a float full of enormous vegetables rolled slowly by, waving to us with gloved hands. After that we saw some more balloons, and finally, when our feet and noses were beginning to get cold, there was Santa in his sleigh, the end of the parade.

"Ho, ho, ho! Merry Christmas!" he called, which I enjoyed hearing, even if Christmas was still weeks away.

By the time we got back home, Mom had the kitchen under control. I finished the place cards, Daddy Bo took a nap, and all in all it was a nice afternoon.

The Lebarros came over at four o'clock, right on time. Justine was wearing a new velvet dress and white tights and slippery black shoes, which she said were tap shoes but really were not. Daddy Bo seemed to have forgotten about going home for Thanksgiving. Instead, he asked eleven times when dinner was going to be served.

The first time he asked, we were all sitting in the family room, even Bitey, and Lexie was passing around a plate of crackers with this disgusting cheese paste. Daddy Bo said, "My, what's that I smell?"

Right away Lexie turned pale, I guess at the very thought that something embarrassing might be said in front of the Lebarros.

I was about to reply that it was probably just the cheese, which smelled like toe sweat, but Daddy Bo answered his own question. "Ah, turkey," he said, turning his head in the direction of the kitchen. "And what time will dinner be served?" He sounded king-like, very grand. Also very happy. The holidays were cheering everyone up.

"Five o'clock," answered Mom.

"We're dining fashionably early then," said Daddy Bo, and he grinned and his chin flap swayed.

I sat down in an armchair and Justine came along and squished herself in next to me. "Let's pretend we know how to talk French," she said. "Too-loo voo-lay fra-la. Sho-nay?"

I stared at her.

"Sho-*nay*?" she said again, more urgently.

Lexie did half an eye roll.

"And what time will we be dining tonight?" said Daddy Bo from the couch.

"He just asked that," Justine whispered to me. "I mean, mee-vroo so-la par-kay."

"Five o'clock," Lexie whispered impatiently in his ear as she passed around the toe-sweat things again.

"Talk *French*," Justine said to me.

"I'd better help pass," I replied, and wiggled out of the chair. I surveyed the dishes on the coffee table and chose one that just had nuts in it. I helped myself to an almond and then began walking around the room, holding out the dish of non-smelly snacks in a proper manner. "Daddy Bo?" I said when I got to the couch.

"Thank you, but I'd better not. I don't want to spoil my dinner. Speaking of which, what time will dinner be served tonight?"

Justine leaped out of the chair. "Five—," she started to say in what seemed to me to be a rather loud voice, but Mr. Lebarro caught hold of her and pulled her into his lap.

Lexie's eyes widened and she blushed deeply. She looked like she wanted to get up and leave, but she didn't and I knew why. It was getting so that I could tell exactly what was going on in her head: If she left, everyone would think she was going to the bathroom, which would be even more embarrassing to her than anything Daddy Bo said. So my sister crossed her arms, stared stonily at the ceiling, and tried to ignore Daddy Bo (and probably Justine and me too).

When dinner was finally served, Daddy Bo sat down at the table, looked at the place cards and all the dishes of food and said, "My goodness. Turkey! How nice. What's the occasion?"

Luckily, Justine didn't hear this. She already had her hands on her popper and was ready to pull the ends. "Can I?" she asked her mother, and pulled without waiting for an answer. *Pop!*

Mom and Dad exchanged a worried glance, but Daddy Bo spread his napkin elegantly in his lap and then graciously passed the bowl of mashed potatoes to Mrs. Lebarro, saying, "Madame?"

So Dad began to carve the turkey and soon we were all wearing paper hats and passing around food, and Daddy Bo was grinning like a Halloween jack-o'-lantern.

Mom and Dad had fixed every Thanksgiving food I like, including stuffing and apple pie. By the time I went to bed that night I wasn't feeling too well.

"Lexie?" I called from the bottom bunk.

"Reading," she replied. Which meant: Don't bother me. And also: Get a book of your own.

"But my stomach hurts."

I heard a sigh from above. "You ate too much."

"I know. It was all so good."

"Try to go to sleep. You'll feel better in the morning." This was the nicest thing my sister had said to me in days.

So I closed my eyes and soon my head was sort of

floaty and drifty, and before I knew it I was at the parade again.

When I woke up, the room was dark and someone was sitting next to me, tapping my shoulder. "Pearl? Are you all right?"

It was my sister. I moaned a little.

"You're not going to barf, are you?" she asked.

"No. I just had a bad dream. We were watching the parade and one of those carrots started chasing me."

"What carrots?"

"The ones on that vegetable float, with the big Mickey Mouse hands."

Lexie laughed softly. "Did the carrot catch you?"

I shook my head. "When you woke me up, I was still running down the sidewalk. But the other vegetables were jumping off the float and heading in our direction."

"How's your stomach?"

"Better." In fact, it was a lot better. "You know what I'm going to have for lunch tomorrow? A turkey sandwich."

"Me too," said Lexie.

Then she climbed back up to the top bunk and I fell asleep thinking about the parade and the Lebarros and the poppers and our feast.

And Daddy Bo's questions.

17

Dear Santa,

Hello! How are you and Mrs. Claus and all the elves and raindeer? By the way is Rudolph <u>really</u> one of your deer because if he is then that makes nine and in The Night Before Christmas there are only eight and he isn't mentioned. Well, it's okay if he isn't real. On the other hand, maybe he just came along later.

What I would like for Christmas is art supplies and pretty much whatever you want to give me. Here's what I'm low on as far as supplies go—papers in nice designs. Also, I would like some more rubber stamps. One thing I do not want is clothes. Clothes are boring. Especially sweaters. Oh, ~~a gift certa cert~~ a gift card to the crafts store would be great.

Your freind, Pearl Littlefield

It is a tradition in my family that Lexie and I write our letters to Santa on December first. Then we hand them over to Mom and Dad to mail. The letters are helpful to them too, for their Christmas shopping, which they always do in a huge rush the week before Christmas.

"What are you asking for?" I said to Lexie as we sat at the table in the family room on the night of December first. Lexie had a ton of homework to do, and also she was supposed to be rehearsing for the middle school orchestra's Winter Concert, but she would never miss writing her Santa letter.

"Well," said Lexie, and for a teensy second I was afraid she was going to say, "I want my private bedroom back." But she didn't. She set her pen down and looked at me. "I have a sort of a problem. And I'm trying to figure out if presents can fix it. . . ."

I felt like I was in the wild and I had just spotted a rare animal, but that if I moved too quickly the animal would dart away. So instead of pouncing on Lexie and shrieking, "You have a problem? Tell me! Tell me!" I turned back to my own letter and said casually, "What's the problem?"

"It's a secret."

My sister had never shared a secret with me. "Oh. Well, you can tell me if you want. Or not. Whatever."

"It's the Emmas," said Lexie after a pause.

"Yeah?"

"They don't invite me places anymore. They ask Valerie to do things, but they don't ask me."

I stared thoughtfully out the window. I knew exactly how Lexie felt, but all I said was, "Hmm."

"I thought maybe if I looked more grown-up—"

"*More* grown-up!" I couldn't help exclaiming.

"I mean, more grown-up than the Emmas, not than you," said Lexie. "If I looked more grown-up, they might start including me again. So I'm asking for makeup and this bracelet I saw in the window of Harmon's and a gift certificate to—"

"How *do* you spell 'certificate'?" I interrupted her.

My sister pointed to the seventh line of her letter.

"Thanks. I'll copy it later."

"Anyway, if I got some new clothes—maybe a nice sweater or something—and some makeup so that I look more sophisticated, well, you know . . ."

I only sort of knew. But since this was the first time in history that my sister had talked to me about a problem I hadn't been the cause of, and I didn't want to ruin the moment, I nodded wisely. "That ought to do the trick," I said.

"I hope so."

Lexie and I finished our letters, and then Dad made hot chocolate and my whole family sat at the table and talked about Christmas.

"We always put our tree right over there," I told Daddy Bo, pointing to a corner of the room near the window.

"Since we don't have a fireplace," added Lexie, "we leave our stockings on the couch."

"When can we get our tree?" I asked.

"Next week," replied Mom.

I felt a little prickle of excitement. Christmas is absolutely my favorite time of the year.

Usually December crawls by so slowly you can't even feel it. But this year it went faster. Daddy Bo came along to help us pick out the tree. Cards started arriving in the mail. I counted my money and made a list of presents to buy for Mom and Dad and Lexie and Daddy Bo.

Then on December 19th a very bad thing happened. At first it was just a regular old afternoon. Justine had come home from school with me and we had spent some time making a Santa hat for Bitey that I knew he would never wear. Then Mom had suggested that I start my homework, so Justine had gone home, but ten minutes later she was back. She stood in our family room with her hands clasped in front of her and right away I knew something bad had happened. I don't know how I knew, but I did.

"What's wrong?" I asked her.

Justine looked down at her shoes. "We're moving," she said finally.

I didn't know what to say to that, so I didn't say anything.

"Daddy came home from work and he and Mom said they wanted to talk to me and that's what they said. 'Justine, we're going to move to a new apartment.'"

"In our building?" I asked, even though I already knew the answer.

Justine shook her head and she had that funny pinched look around her mouth like she was trying not to cry.

"Then . . . where?" I found that I didn't want to look at Justine, so instead I looked at the couch where Bitey was lying on his back with all his feet sticking in the air.

Justine frowned. "We're moving to Seventy-eighth and Amsterdam," she said slowly, as if she were trying out the words.

"Seventy-eighth and Amsterdam!" I wailed. "That's all the way uptown! It isn't near here at all."

Justine's face got even more pinched and she added, "I have to go to a new school. I'll start there after vacation."

"In January? You'll be going to a new school *next month*?" Who was I going to play with during roof time? Who was going to come over after school? What was I going to do without my best friend?

"Yup," said Justine in a small voice. "January."

"Why are you moving?"

"My parents bought a bigger apartment. It's near this school they want me to go to. And they said we can get a dog."

"A dog? What's so great about a dog?" It would probably smell.

Justine shrugged. "I don't know."

There didn't seem to be anything left to say, except maybe, "I hate you, Mr. and Mrs. Lebarro," but of course I couldn't really say that. At least, not in front of Justine.

Justine went back to her apartment and I barged into Lexie's bedroom, where she was doing her homework with the door closed and announced, "I need my alone hour."

Lexie stared at me like I was a roach instead of her sister. "Excuse me, door closed, knocking necessary."

"Sorry, but I need some privacy and this is supposed to be my alone hour."

Lexie jumped up, pushing her chair back, and it almost tipped over. "Pearl, you can't just— Hey, are you crying? What's the matter?"

"I'm not crying!" I wailed, but clearly I was.

"What's the matter?" Lexie asked again, this time in a softer voice. She plunked back down in her chair.

"Nothing!"

"Are you mad at me?"

"Not everything is about you!"

"Okay, okay. I'm just trying to find out what's wrong."

"Nothing! I already said. Can I please have the room?"

Lexie gathered up her books and left, closing the door behind her.

I flung myself onto the bottom bunk and cried. I considered pounding the wall with my shoe, but since technically it was Lexie's wall, I decided I'd better not. I imagined walking to school without Justine, and walking home without Justine, and walking through the halls of Emily Dickinson Elementary without Justine. I imagined roof time with zero people to play with. Who would I go trick-or-treating with? Who would come to my apartment every afternoon?

My life was ruined.

I heard a little creak and lifted my head in time to see the door open.

"Pearl?" said Lexie.

"I do not believe my hour is up. And anyway, what about knocking?"

"You're right. I should have knocked. But Mrs. Lebarro just came over, so I know why you're crying. Can't we talk for a few minutes?"

I shrugged.

The door closed and then I felt the bed shake so I knew Lexie had sat down on the end of it. "You know, Justine isn't moving to Tasmania," said my sister.

"Where's Tasmania?"

Lexie let out a sigh. "Just . . . really far away. She's only moving to the Upper West Side."

"She's *switch*ing to a different *school*."

"I know. But you'll still get to see her."

"Only sometimes. And we'll have to take the *sub*way. I'll probably get to see her, like, once a month."

"I agree, it isn't ideal."

I raised my head and frowned at my sister. "No kidding."

"But think of all the things you can do when you do see Justine. Her new apartment isn't far from the Children's Museum or the Museum of Natural History."

"Justine does like dinosaurs," I said cautiously.

"And you can still have sleepovers. In fact, they'll be more like real sleepovers since you'll get to pack a bag and also probably go out to breakfast in the morning. Really, you'll get to *do* more things, Pearl."

This was true. I sat up. "Thanks," I said.

"You're welcome."

During dinner that night I got an idea, and later, while Lexie was practicing her piece for the Winter Concert,

I sat at our desk with my markers and also some glitter glue and rubber stamps. I made a new sign for the door:

When Lexie saw the sign she said, "That's really nice, Pearl." And she didn't even take it down.

Here's what was wrong with January:

    1. Justine moved. ☹

    2. Christmas was over.

    3. Justine moved.

    4. Lexie was in a bad mood.

    5. Justine moved.

There was more, like without Justine afternoons were as boring as I'd thought they were going to be, and roof time at school was awful. But at least the weather was sloppy and cold so mostly we had recess in our classroom and then James Brubaker the Third and I would draw pictures of Jill and Rachel and Katie with their hair on fire and holes in their clothes and black eyes.

Once Jill saw the pictures by accident and she said, "And who are *they* supposed to be?" And I said, "Oh, just some mean girls. You don't know them." And I could tell Jill didn't believe me, which was actually the point.

The very first day I had to go to school without Justine—when Dad and I walked through the lobby of our building, just the two of us—John looked at me with eyes that were tragic like Lexie's frequently get, but luckily he didn't say anything, not even, "Have a good day," since he knew I wouldn't. Then Dad and I stepped outside and my father reached for my hand as usual, but I pulled it away. I didn't want to hurt his feelings, though, so I said, "Let's see what Snowball is wearing." (Snowball's owner makes him wear doggie coats in the winter.)

We passed by Quik-Mart and New World and Steve-Dan's and finally Happy-Go-Lucky, and next came Alice's stoop, and there she was with Snowball. It was sleeting a little, so this morning Snowball was wearing a red parka, which I think was lined with some sort of fake fur, and on his feet were four tiny yellow rubber boots with black buckles painted on them. Snowball was sitting very still looking like he wanted to die out of embarrassment, and Alice was saying urgently, "Snowball, go make. Go *make*, Snowball!" I glanced up at Dad and we managed to turn the corner before we started laughing.

It felt nice to laugh with Dad, even if it was the first day back at school and Christmas was over and my best friend had moved away. So I decided to take his hand after all, and I held on to it until I realized that Rachel and Katie and Jill and Mrs. DiNunzio were ahead of us.

I stopped in my tracks and let go of his hand.

"Dad, could I walk the rest of the way without you?" I asked. "You can stand back here and watch me if you want." (We were about half a block from the front door of Emily Dickinson.)

"Okay," Dad replied.

He bent over and I knew he was going to kiss my forehead, so before he could, I shook his hand. "Have an enjoyable day at the office, Father," I said.

I ran to catch up with Rachel and Katie and Jill, and was very pleased by the stunned expressions on their faces when they saw that I was alone. They probably thought I had walked to school by myself.

"Hey," I said, and passed right by them on my way to room 4C.

That was fun, but it didn't change anything. By lunchtime the sleet had stopped so we had roof time, and I spent it friendless, which I had only had to do once so far in fourth grade, on a day when Justine was home with a cold. I sat on a bench and watched the kids playing four-square and shooting hoops. Katie and Jill and Rachel must all have gotten the very same hair kit thing for Christmas and Hanukkah because each of them came to recess with a purple flowered bag full of barrettes and scrunchies and braid holders, and during all of roof time they invented hairdos like in a fancy salon.

After school I walked home with Lexie and then spent the afternoon with Daddy Bo, who kept saying, "Why don't you see if Justine can come over?"

So January slogged on. The only good school days were the ones when the weather was bad and James Brubaker the Third and I could spend recess drawing alarming pictures of Katie, etc., etc., etc. At home the afternoons were so boring that I just did my homework, which pleased everyone, except me, since I would rather have been playing with Justine.

One Thursday I sat at the table in the family room, filling out math worksheets and trying to think up a poem about nature. Daddy Bo sat behind me on the couch, studying the rules to Sorry! and reading them aloud, over and over and over and over again.

The front door opened and in walked Lexie. Usually she's talking on her cell phone when she comes home, and usually she's talking to whoever she just spent the afternoon with. Like, downstairs on Twelfth Street she'll say good-bye to Valerie, and as she enters the lobby and passes John's desk she'll snap her phone on and call Valerie so they can continue their conversation. Then Lexie steps onto the elevator and she always has to say, "Wait a sec. I'm on the elevator now," which I guess means that cell phones don't work in elevators, but honestly, why should they? Lexie stands there with the useless phone still at her ear while the elevator huffs up to the seventh floor, and the second she steps into the hall, she goes, "Okay, I'm back," and then she and Valerie keep on talking, and they talk while Lexie comes in the apartment and disappears into her room and closes the door.

But on that Thursday Lexie's ear didn't have a phone stuck to it. And I realized that I hadn't seen much of the phone the last few days. And that Lexie had been quiet at dinner lately. During the time when we were supposed to talk about our days she would just say, "I got an A on a Spanish test," or, "We had a substitute in history." Those were the boring kind of comments I usually made, except that at Emily Dickinson you don't start Spanish until fifth grade.

"Where's Valerie?" I asked, as Lexie marched into the apartment. I hadn't seen much of Valerie the last few days either.

"Don't ask me," said Lexie and stomped away. I noticed that she hadn't been wearing her purple shoes.

On Saturday night Mom and Dad and Daddy Bo went out to dinner. I don't know why it's such a treat for grown-ups to eat in restaurants without their children, since they like family time so much. But anyway they went out, looking all excited and happy, and they hired Lexie to be my babysitter. Which meant she got paid. I myself think both of us should have gotten paid for staying home alone, but whatever.

Lexie took her job seriously. She studied our board games, selected Life, and set it up on the table in the family room. We sat on opposite sides of the board, and Lexie reached for the spinner. I put my chin in my hands and stared at nothing.

"Pearl? What's wrong?" she asked.

I was very sad. "Guess what. Justine won't be here on my birthday." My birthday was months away, over summer vacation.

"She won't?"

I shook my head. "She and her parents are going to go to *Paris*."

"Wow. That's cool."

"No, it isn't! If Justine isn't here, who will come to my party? No one, that's who. And I'm going to be ten. *Ten*. That's double digits. It's a very important birthday, Lexie. Don't you remember your tenth birthday party?"

A funny look came over Lexie's face. Sort of pale and strained like when she didn't want anyone to know how embarrassed she was that I had shown Snuffy to Dallas.

"Well, don't you?" I said. "I do. Valerie came, and the Emmas—"

"I know who was there," replied Lexie, scowling.

"So see? You had guests. And who am I going to have? Just you and Mom and Dad and Daddy Bo and Bitey."

"What's wrong with us?"

"Nothing. It's just, you know. You aren't kids." I slid Life aside. "Let's play later." I found a piece of paper and began a sad letter to Mom about the whole birthday party tragedy.

I had gotten as far as Dear Mom, when I realized that Lexie was just sitting across from me, doing nothing. After a little while, she disappeared, which very soon felt like I was alone in the apartment even though I knew I wasn't, so I went looking for her.

I walked down the hall and saw that the door to our room was closed.

I hesitated. Technically, this was Lexie's alone time, but since Lexie was my babysitter at the moment I decided it would be okay to knock on the door.

No answer.

I knocked again.

When there was still no answer, I opened the door and stuck my head into the room. "Lexie? Could you come out, please? I don't like being in the family room all by myself when—"

I stopped talking. I heard sniffling coming from my

sister's bed. "Lexie?" I called. "What's wrong?" When she *still* didn't answer me I said, "Should I call Mom and Dad at the restaurant?"

Lexie sat up quickly, and I could see that she'd been crying. "No!" she exclaimed. "Don't call them. I'm fine."

"You're crying."

"Something's going on at school."

"Is it that thing with the Emmas?"

"No. That's over. We're friends again. This is something different. But everything is really okay."

"If it's okay, why are you crying?"

"All right, look. I'll tell you what's wrong if you'll just please stop talking about it."

As far as I could see, I hadn't started talking about it, but whatever. I plunked myself down in the desk chair.

"All right," said Lexie again. "On our first day back at school after vacation, this new girl, Lindsey, joined our grade. She's in my homeroom, and Mr. Fourtney"— here I almost yelped, "Mr. Fartney?" but luckily I kept my mouth closed—"who's my guidance counselor," continued Lexie, "asked me if I'd be Lindsey's buddy and show her around school for a week. So I did. I walked her to her classes and showed her where the cafeteria and the library and everything are, and then I introduced her to Dallas and Valerie and the Emmas and everyone so that she would have friends too."

"That was nice of you," I said.

"I thought so. But then Lindsey and Valerie started spending all their time together, like . . . like best friends." (Lexie's voice wobbled.) "And now they leave me out of things and they're always on the phone with each other. If I call Valerie she just says, 'I can't talk now, Lexie. I'm on with Lindsey.' Which is *so rude*. She doesn't even say, 'I'll call you right back.'"

"You know what you should do?" I exclaimed suddenly. "You should invite both of them to a sleepover or to go to the movies with you or something."

I could tell that Lexie was turning this idea over in her mind, even though she didn't want to, since it had come from me. But at last she said, "Both of them? Valerie and Lindsey together? Well, maybe."

I felt inspired. I saw a pad of paper on the desk and I handed it up to Lexie along with a pen. "Make a list of things you and Valerie and Lindsey could do," I said, like I was Mr. Potter giving an assignment. Then I went back to the family room, which didn't seem so creepy now, and I finished my letter to Mom. I planned to leave it under her pillow before I went to bed. I wrote:

First things first, can you please get
someone to come to my birthday party since
Justine won't be here. Next can you please

get me my own cell phone or key to the apartment because nobody is coming to my birthday party.

I am having a great time with Lexie so I hope you are having fun with Dad and Daddy Bo.

Love, Pearl

P.S. How was the food?

P.P.S. How was the restaurant?

P.P.P.S. I would like to ~~con congr~~ say good job for finishing your latest book!

P.P.P.P.S. I also want my own computer since nobody is coming to my birthday party.

P.P.P.P.P.S. I have never written this many P.S.s in my whole life.

Love again, your daughter Pearl Littlefield

19

The days went by and even though it was flu season, nobody in our family caught it. But Mr. Potter caught it 2x so we had a lot of substitute teachers, and then John got it too so we also had a substitute doorman, and I think Mrs. Mott might have caught it because things were peaceful around the building and all the dog owners took their dogs in the regular elevator.

One day I was sitting at Lexie's desk starting my homework, which was to keep a journal for a week. This had been assigned by our current substitute, who clearly didn't realize that fourth graders have nothing whatsoever to write about. Mr. Potter would have known this, but the substitute didn't. She must have been used to substituting at Lexie's school, where the kids can write about boyfriends and talking on their cell phones and letting themselves into their apartments with their own keys. But what was I going to write about? Bitey?

I was still trying to think what to say when I heard the door to Mom's office open and a moment later she stuck her head in the room and said, "Pearl, I'm having a problem with my computer. I think I need to take it over to the computer store."

"Okay," I replied.

"What I mean is that you'll have to come with me. Lexie isn't here."

"Can't I stay home with Daddy Bo?"

Mom hesitated. "Well—"

"*Please?*" I begged. There is nothing worse than hanging around the computer store while Mom gets all anxious and frustrated waiting for her turn to talk with a technician. "I promise I'll do my homework," I said. "Look, I'm starting it already." I pointed to my notebook. "We have to keep a journal."

"All right," said Mom at last. And then she added, "Pearl, I'm very pleased with how responsible you've been lately."

"Thank you," I said politely, although everyone knew the main reason I'd been so responsible lately was because Justine was gone and I was bored.

"I'll be back in less than an hour," Mom continued, frowning. She looked like she wasn't sure she'd made the right decision. But then I heard her in the office saying, "Turn on. Turn *on*!" which meant she was talking to her useless computer. The next thing I knew she was closing the apartment door behind her.

I stared at the blank notebook in front of me. Finally, at the top of the first page, in the very middle, I wrote: My Journal. I stared a little longer and on the next line, on the right side, I added: Monday, January 24. I had absolutely no idea what to write next, so I was relieved when Daddy Bo appeared in the doorway.

But I was surprised when he said, "Pearl, put on your coat. We're going to New Jersey."

"What? What do you mean?"

"I mean we have to go to New Jersey. Right now. It's high time I went back to my house for a visit."

"But, Daddy Bo, I have to work on this journal," I said, at the same time thinking how lame my assignment was going to be, even if it was for a substitute. If I went to New Jersey, at least I would have something to write about.

Daddy Bo was already wearing his coat. And he was holding mine out to me with a pleading look in his eyes. In my head I started going, "Lame journal, trip to New Jersey. Lame journal, trip to New Jersey."

The trip to New Jersey won out.

"Okay," I said. I put my coat on, and we left the apartment.

I waited in the hallway for Daddy Bo to fish his keys out of his pocket so he could lock our door, but he was already heading for the elevator. That should have been a little clue that there was a problem. But I needed an adventure for my journal, and besides, Daddy Bo looked desperate, and besides *that*, it's really hard to tell a grown-up what to do.

"Daddy Bo? We better lock the door!" I said. I tried to sound excited, like his mistake was just another feature of the adventure.

"Whoops," he said, and went back inside to find his keys.

A few minutes later we had had a nice, quiet, Mrs. Mott-free ride downstairs and were stepping into the lobby, when I had a sudden memory of the afternoon John had called me to collect Daddy Bo. I took a look at my grandfather and tried to see if he'd remembered everything I had included on the list I'd made for him that day. I couldn't tell about his underwear, of course, and I didn't know if his wallet was in his pocket, but he seemed to have everything else he needed, including shoes, which was a relief.

We passed by the doorman station and I said hello to the guy who was standing there even though I didn't know his name. He smiled at us and held the door open, and what do you know—Daddy Bo stepped right out onto Twelfth Street, stuck his arm in the air, and in an

instant a taxi had pulled over. Daddy
expert. Even my parents never hailed cal

I began to feel better about our adven

"Port Authority, please," said Daddy F
(Port Authority is the bus station, which
there too many times since we have our green Subaru.)
Then Daddy Bo turned to me and said, "Buckle up, Pearl."

We snapped our seat belts in place.

Daddy Bo was acting like a responsible adult.

I looked out the window of the cab as the driver turned right onto Fifth Avenue, right again onto Eleventh Street, and right once again onto Sixth Avenue. On Sixth, we crawled uptown for a while and soon we had passed all of my familiar landmarks and were in a different neighborhood.

"It's the perfect day for an adventure, isn't it, Pearl?" said Daddy Bo.

The sky was cloudy and the afternoon was gloomy and a man on the curb had just shaken his fist at our driver and yelled something rude to him, but I guess Daddy Bo hadn't noticed any of those things.

"Yup," I replied.

After that none of us said anything until the driver stopped the cab and turned around to face us.

"Oh, are we here?" asked Daddy Bo.

The driver was very nice and didn't say, "Duh," although he could have. Instead he answered, "Yes, sir."

Bo fished his wallet out of his pocket, so I
my list had been useful. He paid the driver, and
ı pretty sure he included a tip.

We stepped onto the sidewalk, which was very crowded
with people. In fact, it was much more crowded than
the sidewalks around Twelfth Street, and as Daddy Bo
hurried toward the entrance to the Port Authority building I grabbed the back of his coat so we wouldn't get
separated. Daddy Bo was walking fast, even through the
crowd, and when I could finally look at his face I realized that he wasn't thinking of anything except the bus
ride to New Jersey.

"Daddy Bo?" I said nervously. It was starting to get
dark out.

"Oh, there you are, Pearl. Good. Now, let's see."
Daddy Bo pulled me into the bus station, which was
quite large, and after standing and thinking for a while,
with people streaming all around us and sometimes
bumping us with their briefcases and shopping bags
and not stopping to apologize, he finally said, "Over
there, Pearl."

He headed for a row of ticket machines, found a free
one, and stood in front of it for quite some time, studying the choices and directions and watching the people
using the machines on either side of him. Finally a
woman from behind us said, "Hello, are you going to
use that machine?"

Daddy Bo turned around with a sort of cross expression on his face, but then he said in a dignified manner, "I was, but I didn't realize I'd need a degree from MIT to operate it."

I didn't know what MIT was, and I have a feeling the lady didn't either, but she smiled nicely and said, "I think these things are complicated too. If you want, you can go to a ticket window and talk to an actual person." She pointed across the station.

Daddy Bo smiled back at her and said thank you, and we headed off in a different direction. We made our way through the crowds, which by the way, felt like we were in a rushing river, not that I have ever actually been in one. As we hurried along, I said, "Hey, Daddy Bo? Do you have enough money for our tickets?" I thought he might say no, and that would be the end of the adventure. If he didn't have enough money to take a cab back to our apartment either, we would be stuck at the bus station, but at least we would still be in New York.

Daddy Bo didn't even need to look in his wallet, though. He just said, "Oh, I certainly do."

And he did.

At the window he bought two tickets to New Jersey and found out which gate our bus would leave from. "You only have ten minutes," added the ticket man.

"We'd better hurry then, Pearl," said Daddy Bo.

Now a very uncomfortable feeling was settling over

me. Mom would probably return from the computer store soon, and I realized that Daddy Bo and I hadn't left her a note. Plus, it would be completely dark by the time we reached Daddy Bo's old house. And *plus*, I had noticed that Daddy Bo had only bought one-way tickets to New Jersey. Round-trip tickets would have been better. But maybe he couldn't afford them.

"Daddy Bo? How are we going to get home?" I asked as we stepped onto a very long escalator. "Do you have enough money for more tickets?"

Daddy Bo didn't answer until we were at the top of the escalator. Then all he said was, "Blimey, Pearl! We will soon away!"

Which made no sense at all.

Daddy Bo was looking at his watch now and pulling me along behind him. Out of the corner of my eye I noticed a police officer. Even though the first thought that jumped into my mind was what happened after I yelled "Help, police!" in the Museum of Natural History, leading to the third of the Three Bad Things, I thought maybe I should tell the officer what was happening now. This problem seemed a little more serious. There were the one-way tickets and no note for Mom and the fact that I was pretty sure Daddy Bo's house was empty, since my parents said they had moved his things into storage.

I tried to imagine how the conversation with the officer would go.

"Excuse me, ma'am?" I would say. "I'm with my grandfather and he's taking me to New Jersey but my parents don't know anything about it."

This sounded so bad that I couldn't even think what the officer might do. All I knew was that Daddy Bo would be in huge, enormous trouble.

If I had a cell phone I could have called Mom or Dad. But of course I didn't have one. Neither did Daddy Bo. I felt around in the pockets of my jeans. I didn't have any money either. Then I thought, Daddy Bo is my *grand*father. He loves me. How bad could this be?

"Here we are!" said Daddy Bo, coming to a stop at last.

We joined the end of a line of people boarding a bus. Daddy Bo clutched our tickets and smiled as happily as if we were waiting for the Cinderellabration at Disney World. Soon we were climbing on the bus ourselves, and we found two seats together not far from the driver. I looked around at the other passengers, who were talking on their cell phones and sending text messages, and I decided that when I wrote out my birthday list for Mom and Dad, #1 on the list would be: My own cell phone IN CASE OF EMERGENCIES. Did you know I could even use it to call you FROM A BUS? A cell phone is a great tool for STAYING OUT OF TROUBLE.

I started to think about the rest of my list, since dreaming about presents is always fun, and since Daddy

Bo seemed to be very, very far away even though he was sitting right next to me. Once I turned to him and said, "Daddy Bo, where are we?" and he grinned and replied, "We're in New Jersey, Pearl!"

First of all, duh. And second of all, why did he sound as if he had just said, "We're in the magic land of Narnia, Pearl," instead of what he had actually said?

I looked out the window. We were passing by some horribly ugly places, full of fuel tanks and smokestacks. Pardon me for saying so, but the bus began to fill up with a very bad smell, which was not coming from anything *on* the bus, so it must have been coming from those factories, or whatever they were. Daddy Bo didn't seem to notice either the scenery or the smell, though. He just sat next to me with a little smile on his face. And after a while we pulled into a town that, even in the dark, I could tell was pretty.

Daddy Bo's smile widened, the driver began to make stops, letting people off the bus, and soon Daddy Bo rose to his feet and said, "We're almost there, Pearl."

Even though the trip was exciting and I was pleased that I would have something to write about in my diary, I realized that I didn't want to get off the bus. It seemed like a nice, safe place, with the driver in charge of things. But I had to follow Daddy Bo, and a few minutes later we stepped onto a sidewalk and the bus pulled away, and my grandfather and I were all alone in the darkness.

I reached for Daddy Bo's hand.

"Hmm," said Daddy Bo, looking around.

I looked around too. It had been a while since I had visited Daddy Bo. I tried to figure out if we were on his street, but it was hard to tell in the dark. I saw houses and mailboxes and trees and fences, but they could have been houses and mailboxes and trees and fences on any street in any town. I didn't want to appear stupid, but finally I said, "Is this your street?"

There was a short pause before Daddy Bo replied, "Well, it must be. Yes, I think so." And then, "We'll be at my house in no time. I think."

He didn't sound very confident, but we walked along anyway through the dim light of the streetlamps. After a while Daddy Bo picked up his pace and I had to run to keep up with him. As we passed under streetlamps I could see my breath, and I realized that my hands and my nose were very cold.

"Are we on the right track?" I asked finally, stuffing my free hand in my pocket.

"Absolutely."

We passed houses with porches and yards and gardens. The houses looked friendly enough, but no one was on the street except Daddy Bo and me, and I got a creepy feeling, like I was a character in a scary movie my parents had told me not to watch. Luckily, even though our trip seemed to take forever, we hadn't walked more than two more blocks before Daddy Bo said, "Here we are!" and suddenly I recognized his neat white house with the wide front window.

I didn't answer him, though. This was because all at once Daddy Bo and I both noticed the same thing: Stuck in the middle of the front yard was a FOR SALE sign, and slapped across it was a sticker that said SOLD.

Daddy Bo began to cry.

20

"Maybe this isn't my house after all," said Daddy Bo. He was sniffing, and wiping his eyes with a handkerchief, and I was holding his hand tightly. I really wanted him to stop crying. This was worse than when Lexie had cried while she was babysitting for me. "Maybe in the dark I got confused," he added.

"Let's check," I said. I tried to remember Daddy Bo's address from when I used to send him postcards. Number 29 Blake Road. I peered at the mailbox at the end of the driveway. In the light from one of the streetlamps I could plainly see the silver 29 on the side of the box. "Okay, well, it *is* your hou—"

But Daddy Bo wasn't listening to me. He began talking again before I had finished my sentence. "How can I come home if my house has been sold?"

I gazed up at my grandfather. Mom and Dad had been talking about finding a new home for Daddy Bo since the moment Dad had come back from visiting him in the hospital, which was way before Halloween. How could Daddy Bo think he would be moving here again?

Then I remembered all the things Daddy Bo had been forgetting lately, like how to play Sorry! and what his chin flap was for and that he needed to wear shoes when leaving the apartment. So maybe he'd forgotten about the conversations with my parents. Or maybe he just hadn't wanted to believe that he couldn't come home again. Not even for a visit.

I realized that if the house had been sold, all Daddy Bo could do now was stand in the dark and look at it. He couldn't go inside, even though it had been his home for more than forty years.

What do you know, Daddy Bo interrupted those exact thoughts to say, "Well, we can still get inside. I'll just use the spare key."

"What? We're going inside? What spare key?" I was completely startled, and a little frightened. "Daddy Bo, we can't go inside if it's been sold. That means the house belongs to someone else now. I think we would be trespassing."

In my mind I saw a cartoon hillbilly with wild hair and whiskers on his chin nailing a falling-apart wooden

NO TRESPASSING sign to a dead tree. A vulture was sitting in the tree, and I could hear the hammer banging and see the furious expression on the hillbilly's face, which plainly said that if anyone ignored the sign he would come after the *trespasser* with a sledgehammer and maybe an anvil.

"How can you trespass on your own property?" was Daddy Bo's reply.

"But it *isn't* your property. Anymore." I said this breathlessly because once again I was running to keep up with Daddy Bo. For an old person who had recently had an accident and hurt himself, he could move awfully fast. "Where are you going?"

"To get the key." Daddy Bo said this as if I had just asked him something ridiculous like what my own name was.

"But we can't go inside!" I was starting to feel panicky now. Still, I followed Daddy Bo around to the back of the house. I didn't want to be left alone in the dark.

Daddy Bo stepped onto the back stoop and reached up to feel along the ledge above the door. "Huh," he said after a few moments. He moved over and felt along the other end of the ledge. "Where *is* it?"

I was trying hard to keep up with whatever was going on in Daddy Bo's mind. "The key?" I asked.

"Of course the key."

"But, Daddy Bo, if the house has been sold maybe the new owner doesn't keep the key here anymore. And maybe the key wouldn't fit the door now anyway."

"Why wouldn't the key fit the door?"

"Well, after Justine moved away, the super changed the locks on their door. So maybe—"

Daddy Bo wasn't listening to me. He was walking around to the garage. Both doors were down. He tried to pull them up, first one, then the other. They wouldn't budge.

He continued around to the front yard and walked right up to the door, and I realized that in the light from the streetlamp anybody could see us standing on the porch.

"Daddy Bo," I said in a loud whisper, "I really don't think we should be doing this. We have to go home." I was trying not to cry. "How are we going to do that, anyway? How are we going to get back home? Where do we buy bus tickets at night?"

"I *am* home, Pearl," said Daddy Bo.

"No. You're not. This isn't your house anymore. You live with Mom and Dad and Lexie and me now." I was going to add that sometime soon he would have yet another home, but it didn't seem like the right time to remind him about that, and anyway my teeth were chattering and it was hard to talk.

Daddy Bo and I sat on the top step of the porch. I was trying not to pay too much attention to the darkness, since I didn't know what might be in it, like murderers or snakes, but mostly I felt bad for Daddy Bo. I put my arm across his shoulders. He didn't say anything for a long time. Then slowly he turned to me, and I could see that his face was crumpling like Justine's used to do when she was about to burst into tears.

"I can't even look inside," he said. "I don't have my keys or—" He paused. "I wonder where my car is."

I was pretty sure it had been sold.

Daddy Bo began to gaze around the yard and the driveway. "How did this happen?" he asked at last.

I sighed. It was such a long story.

I sat with my arm around Daddy Bo for a while longer, my nose growing colder and colder, and then I noticed the lights in the house next door, and all of a sudden I remembered that Daddy Bo's friend, Will Henderson, lived there. I got an idea.

"Hey, Daddy Bo," I said. "As long as we're here, why don't we visit Mr. Henderson?"

"Will?" he replied, and he brightened.

I got to my feet and held out my hand. "Yeah. Come on. You haven't seen him in a long time. I bet he'd like a visit."

So Daddy Bo stood up stiffly and took my hand. He

let me lead him across the lawn to Will Henderson's porch. I rang the bell. A few moments later I heard footsteps, and then the curtain by the door parted and a face peered out at us. First the face was frowning, then the mouth opened into a surprised O, and then Will Henderson started to smile.

He unlocked the door and threw it open.

"Well, if you two aren't a sight for sore eyes!" he exclaimed, but he was looking at me with a question mark. Still, he said, "Come in, come in!"

Daddy Bo and I walked through the door and sat on a couch in the living room. "Um, Mr. Henderson," I said. "I'm really thirsty. Could I have a glass of water? I mean, if it isn't too rude to ask."

"Not at all, Pearl. Come with me."

We left Daddy Bo sitting slumped on the couch. Mr. Henderson closed the kitchen door behind us and right away I started talking. "Daddy Bo and I were home alone," I began, trying to think how to explain my problem in a clear way that Mr. Potter would approve of. "And he said 'Let's go to New Jersey,' and it's really hard to say no to a grown-up, so we got in a cab, and everything sort of seemed okay, except I remembered that we hadn't left a note for Mom, and then we took the bus here and it was dark, and Daddy Bo didn't know his house had been sold—"

Mr. Henderson put his hand on my shoulder. "It's

okay, Pearl. I think I understand what happened. Let's call your parents."

"That's another thing. If I had a *cell phone*, I could have called them already. But I'm not allowed to have one."

Mr. Henderson wasn't listening. He was already punching in numbers on his phone. "Paul?" I heard him say. "It's Will Henderson. Pearl and your father are here." This was followed by a long silence. I wondered if my father was crying with relief, and whether, when *he* cried, *his* face crumpled like Justine's.

Mr. Henderson spoke to Dad for a few minutes, then to Mom, and then he handed the phone to me.

My mother was on the other end and *she* was crying. I said, "Yes, I'm fine, I'm fine," over and over again. Then I told her, "We took the bus. . . . Well, he had enough money for one-way tick— . . . No, really, I'm *fine*. Well, actually, I'm hungry. Can we get a pizza for dinner?"

An hour and a half later our green Subaru pulled up at Mr. Henderson's. If I may say so, it was traveling kind of fast for just being on a driveway. It stopped a few inches from the back of Mr. Henderson's Toyota and I heard the brakes screech, which my father has always said is a sign of unnecessary speed. In a flash, both of the front doors and one of the back doors of the Subaru opened, and Mom and Dad and Lexie scrambled out and all ran along Mr. Henderson's walk. I opened the door before they could ring the bell, and for a moment no one said anything. Then Mom hugged me and cried, and Dad stepped inside and hugged Daddy Bo and cried, and Lexie looked at me and I think maybe she wanted to cry, but she didn't, and I didn't either, because I was still thinking about pizza.

By the time we got home that night it was after nine o'clock. I had never eaten dinner so late, not even on New Year's Eve. "Do I have to go to school tomorrow?" I asked.

"Yes," Mom answered.

A few minutes later, when Dad had taken Daddy Bo back to his room, Mom added, "Pearl, what you did today was . . ." She paused. "Well, you did everything right."

If I had really done everything right we probably wouldn't have wound up in New Jersey, but I didn't feel I should interrupt my mother.

"You kept your head," Mom continued. "You didn't panic. You got help from an adult you could trust. And you did it all without embarrassing Daddy Bo or hurting his feelings."

"Thank you," I said. I looked at the clock on the cable box and chewed a piece of pepperoni. "I know it's almost my bedtime, but could I do one of my homework assignments now?" I asked.

My mother looked startled, which was not surprising. "What? Right now? Well, of course. But just one assignment. I'll write a note to your teacher about the others."

A few minutes later Lexie was lying in the top bunk and I was sitting at the desk, my blank journal open in front of me. I had read other journals and knew that you don't always have to put journal thoughts in complete sentences, so I wrote:

Big adventure today. Took bus to state of New Jersey! Was with Daddy Bo and on way to bus station crazy person yelled at our cab driver, "Who taught you to drive? Your grandma?" My grandmother was very good driver when alive, but whatever.

On bus everyone had cell phones, which they didn't work in tunnel though.

Certain parts of NJ smell bad, others are nice.

By the time I stopped writing Lexie was already asleep. I closed the journal, picked up Bitey, and pulled him into bed with me.

21

"Lexie?" I said softly.

"Yeah?"

Lexie was lying in the top bunk, and I was lying in the bottom bunk with Bitey, and the lights were out. It was almost Valentine's Day. That was how much time had passed since my adventure with Daddy Bo. And during those weeks, neither Daddy Bo nor I had been allowed to stay home alone, or home alone together. I had kind of hoped maybe I could become Daddy Bo's babysitter, but no one else thought much of that idea.

"Do you still make valentines for your friends?" I asked my sister.

"Well . . . no."

"You mean you grew out of it?"

"I guess. But I'm going to make a valentine for Dallas."

"Is he going to make one for you?"

"I hope so."

It was on the tip of my tongue to ask, "Are you and Dallas in love?" but I had learned that some of my questions should not get out in the open. Instead I said, "Lexie? Do you think Daddy Bo will like his new home?"

"I don't know. Mom and Dad said he will."

"Yeah. But do *you* think he'll like it?"

"I haven't seen it yet, Pearl."

So far only Mom and Dad had seen it. A week ago the phone had rung and it was this man saying that Daddy Bo's name had come up on the waiting list for a retirement community called The Towers. It was the one on the Upper West Side that Mom and Dad had liked so much.

"You'll have your own suite of rooms, Dad," Mom had told Daddy Bo at dinner that night. "Three rooms all to yourself."

"And we'll be just a subway ride away," my father had added.

"You can eat in the dining room at The Towers so you'll never have to cook," said Mom. "And there's a barber shop and a gift shop and a library and a lecture room. All in one building. You can watch movies or take classes. You can even go on field trips."

This kind of reminded me of the talk my parents had had with me when I was afraid to go to kindergarten.

Now I said to Lexie, "I *hope* Daddy Bo likes The Towers."

"Me too. Hey, Pearl, guess what I found out today. The Towers is only four blocks from Justine's new building."

"Really? Maybe Justine and I will get to see each other more often after Daddy Bo moves." Despite what all the parents had said, Justine and I had seen each other exactly 3x since January. (Also, the Lebarros had not gotten a dog, smelly or otherwise.)

"And you know what else? You'll get your room back," added Lexie.

"So will you."

"Yeah."

"Yeah."

For a few moments, neither of us said anything. Bitey pawed at my covers, so I lifted them up and he crawled underneath and curled up on top of my legs, which I have to tell you made me get sweaty almost immediately, but I was afraid to move him. Finally I said, "Lexie? What if Daddy Bo forgets he's going to move to the new place?"

It turned out that this was why Daddy Bo and I had taken our trip to New Jersey. Mom and Dad *had* told him about his house. They'd told him that he needed to live in a retirement community, and that they were going to sell his house and car, and that his furniture had been put into storage until they could decide how much of it he would need in his new home. They had told him these things slowly, bit by bit, with lots of time in between each new piece of information to give him a chance to adjust. But just like I'd thought, he had forgotten anyway. Or else he hadn't wanted to believe what he was hearing.

It also turned out that my parents had *not* yet told Daddy Bo that his house had actually been sold. But they were getting ready to tell him. I don't think it would have made much difference, though. The other day I saw him studying the map of the building that I had made him, so I knew his memory could use a little help.

"What if he forgets?" Lexie repeated.

"Yeah. Like he forgot all the other things Mom and Dad told him."

"Well, I don't think he forgets things completely. He has good days when he remembers, and bad days when he forgets, and then good days when he remembers again. So I think we should just keep talking about his new place. That will help him remember."

I threw my covers back and tried to air out my legs. Bitey growled softly.

"What's going on down there?" asked Lexie.

"Bitey's making me sweat."

Lexie laughed.

She seemed to be in a good mood, so I said, "Hey,

what's happening with Valerie and Lindsey?" I actually already had a very good idea what was happening since I had discovered that if I stood on the toilet in our bathroom and put my ear up to the heating duct I could hear every word Lexie said on the phone during her alone hour in the bedroom. (I did this with the bathroom door closed, of course, and twice in the last week Mom had almost made me take Pepto-Bismol.)

"Well," said my sister, "first I asked Valerie and Lindsey if they wanted to go to the movies with me one Saturday, and they both said no, they were busy. I knew they were busy doing something together without me, so then I said, 'Okay, when *aren't* you busy?' They could have been really mean and said, 'Never.' But they didn't. So we went to the movies the next weekend. But after *that*, things went back to the way they'd been before."

This was a very long answer to my question.

"So then," Lexie continued, "one day I said, 'Do you want to eat lunch with me tomorrow?' And Valerie said . . ."

At this point, I kind of lost track of my sister's answer. Partly because I had already heard all this stuff in the bathroom when she would call Dallas to report on her life, and partly because, if you must know, it was a teensy bit boring.

I lay in bed, trying not to sweat, and thought about

how Mr. Potter was finally over the flu, and how Jill had caught a different kind of flu and had barfed on her desk in front of everybody in our class (I heard the word "barf" a lot more often these days than I heard about Show and Tell or tinkle or Help, police). And I thought about the fact that no one was coming to my birthday party. Then in my head I started to think about the valentines I wanted to make for my family and Justine, and I was wondering if Mom or Dad could take me to the crafts store soon for supplies, when I realized Lexie was saying, "Pearl? Are you still awake?"

I didn't want my sister to know that I hadn't been listening to her, so I said, "Mmphh, um, yeah," like I had drifted off for a few seconds.

"Well, don't you?" said Lexie.

"Don't I what?"

"Don't you think it's time you had a new best friend?"

"A new best friend?" I pretended to wake up completely. "No! Justine is my best friend. She always will be!"

"Calm down," said Lexie. "All right then, don't you think you should find *another* friend? One who lives nearby, who you can see every day?"

"Well, it isn't like going to the store. You can't just point to somebody and say, 'I want that one.'"

"Of course not. But you do know you can have more

than one friend, don't you? Take me, for instance. Valerie is my best friend. Just like Justine is yours," Lexie added quickly. "And then I'm also friends with the Emmas and Lindsey and Chloe and everyone."

What I wanted to say to Lexie was, "You don't have to brag." But I didn't.

"So," Lexie continued, "who in your class do you have the most fun with?"

I was about to say something mean about Katie and Rachel and Barfy Jill, but to my own surprise, I replied, "James Brubaker the Third." I was thinking of the pictures we had drawn of Jill and Katie and Rachel with their hair on fire.

"The kid across the street?" said Lexie.

"Yeah."

"Okay."

"Okay, what?"

"Okay, then he should be your friend."

"But he's a *boy*."

"So? Justine's your best friend and she's, well, younger. A friend can be a boy or a girl or any age. It doesn't matter if James is a boy."

"James Brubaker the Third," I said. "That's his whole name."

"Well?" said Lexie. "Why don't you invite him over or something?"

"I'll think about it."

So I thought about it and two days later I asked James Brubaker the Third if he wanted to come to my house, and he said he had to ask his parents, so he did, and his mother called my mother and they got things all arranged. On Wednesday, he walked home with Lexie and me, and the very first thing he did was stand in our family room and point across the street to his own building.

"There's my living room window," he announced.

"Cool," I said. "We should write giant notes and hold them up for each other to read."

"We should invent a secret code."

Daddy Bo wandered into the family room then and James Brubaker the Third said, "Hello, Mr. Bo. Where's your tail?"

Daddy Bo smiled and left the room. A few minutes later he came back with the squirrel tail hanging out the back of his pants and asked about James Brubaker the Third's molar costume. I was a little surprised that Daddy Bo remembered the molar costume, which just went to show that Lexie was right about his memory.

"It had a little accident," my new friend admitted. "My dad sucked part of it up the vacuum cleaner, and that was the end of it."

James Brubaker the Third and I got out my art supplies and sat at the table in the family room. I drew a portrait of Bitey, and JBIII told me he thought I was the best artist in our class. He stayed for two hours and he never once mentioned Show and Tell or tinkle or Help, police. When he was leaving, he said, "Go wait at your window, okay?"

I stood at the window in our family room and a few minutes later I saw a light come on in JBIII's window. He waved to me.

I waved back.

That night I got out my comparison chart. I studied the "Friends" line. I thought for a while, and then under Justine's name I added: James Brubaker the Third (boy).

22

I stood in our front hallway and looked at the boxes stacked there, and at Daddy Bo's suitcases. Bitey had jumped up on one of the suitcases, and was sitting straight and tall, licking his paw.

We had had a busy morning. Mom and Dad had helped Daddy Bo pack up the last of his belongings, and then we had all walked through the apartment to see if he'd missed anything.

"If you did, we'll bring it by very soon," Dad said now. "We'll be visiting you often."

Daddy Bo nodded. He was wandering around the family room looking like he didn't know what to do with himself.

"Dad?" said my mother. "Do you remember what today is?"

"Moving day?" replied Daddy Bo. He did not sound very sure.

"That's right. You're moving to your new apartment in The Towers."

"But where's my furniture?"

"It's already there," my father reminded him. "These are just the last few things." He waved toward the boxes in the hall. "Ready to go?"

"I suppose."

Daddy Bo did not sound happy, and I couldn't blame him. Even though Mom and Dad had been talking about what a nice place The Towers was, I kept thinking about nursing homes I'd seen on TV. I pictured old people—rows of them—sleeping in chairs with their mouths open while a big TV played loudly even though nobody was watching it. I pictured people wearing bibs and being fed applesauce like babies, and wandering up and down hallways in their slippers, and asking visitors if they knew how to get to the Statue of Liberty, or telling anyone who would listen that they used to be President Lincoln's secretary and then politely wondering if they could borrow a subway token, which you don't even need tokens for the subway anymore.

This did not sound like the kind of place for Daddy Bo. But it was too late now. His new apartment was ready for him.

Daddy Bo said good-bye to Bitey, who nearly bit him, and then my whole family loaded the boxes and suitcases into our green Subaru and drove uptown. As we passed the Port Authority bus station, Daddy Bo said, "Remember our trip to New Jersey, Pearl? That was fun."

"It was an adventure," I replied, and thought about the A I had gotten on my journal, even though at first the substitute hadn't believed my story.

We drove around Columbus Circle, where my father started yelling things like, "Stay in your own lane!" and then turning to my mother and adding, "He thinks he's so special, he should get two lanes." Dad was about to honk his horn, but my mother reminded him that he could get a fine for that, so instead he shouted, "The light is green! It's *green*! What are you waiting for?" even though all our windows were closed and we were the only ones who could hear him.

I smiled at Daddy Bo and took his hand.

We were all relieved when we finally pulled up in front of a very tall building with a brass plaque next to the front doors that said THE TOWERS.

"Here we are!" said my mother gaily like we had arrived at the circus.

The next half an hour was busy and a little confusing, but when it was over, someone had helped us unload

Daddy Bo's things from the car, and we had ridden the elevator to his apartment on the fifth floor, and already, I had changed my mind about The Towers. I had not seen one person shuffling around in slippers or talking about Abraham Lincoln or the Statue of Liberty.

Plus, Daddy Bo's apartment was really nice.

"Look!" I exclaimed. "All your own furniture." Daddy Bo and I walked from the living room to the den to his bedroom and then peeked in the bathroom. (I noticed that Daddy Bo didn't have a kitchen—just a teensy little area with a refrigerator and a sink, which I decided was a good idea, since he wasn't always reliable with the stove.)

In the living room were the couch and armchairs and coffee table from Daddy Bo's house in New Jersey. In the den were his bookshelves and desk and another armchair. In his bedroom were his bed and his dresser.

"Hey, Daddy Bo, there's already stuff in your closets!" I said. "How did this get here?"

It turned out that my dad had spent some time during the last week getting Daddy Bo's apartment ready.

My mother started opening the boxes we'd brought with us. After a few minutes she looked up and said, "Lexie, why don't you and Pearl and Daddy Bo take a walk around The Towers and see what's what?"

"What are you and Dad going to do?" I asked.

"Stay here and finish unpacking," replied Mom.

I looked at Daddy Bo. A tour sounded like fun. "We can pretend we're explorers," I said to my grandfather.

The three of us stepped out into the hall, which was carpeted, and reminded me of the halls in our apartment building. I looked up and down at all the doors with numbers and letters on them.

"You have lots of neighbors," I told Daddy Bo.

"It's just like our apartment building," added Lexie, and since this was exactly what I had been thinking, I said, "Pinky swear of the brain!"

But no one knew what I meant, and anyway, Daddy Bo had just gotten a look at the nurses' station at the end of the hall, and he said, "There aren't any *nurses* where you live."

He got in a better mood, though, after we'd taken the elevator to the first floor.

"Hey, here's the gift shop!" exclaimed Lexie. There's nothing like shopping to capture her attention.

"Oh, and look, a coffee shop," I said.

A woman sitting at a desk by the front door smiled at us and said, "Mr. Littlefield?"

"Yes?" Daddy Bo answered cautiously.

"Good morning. I'm Harriet Sutton. I work here on the weekends. Welcome to The Towers. Are you taking a tour?"

"We're explorers," I said.

"If you go down that hallway," said Harriet, pointing,

"you'll find the library and the lecture room. On the second floor are the exercise room, the barber shop and beauty parlor, the crafts room—"

"Crafts room!" I cried.

"Yes, you can take classes—"

"Daddy Bo, you can take art classes here!"

My sister pulled me aside and whispered, "Calm down, Pearl."

But I couldn't. "*I* want to live here!" I said.

Finally Daddy Bo smiled. "Sorry. I'm afraid only old gents like me can live here. Well, old gents and old ladies."

We left Harriet and walked along the hall toward the library. Posted on a bulletin board were sign-up sheets for field trips.

"'The Metropolitan Museum of Art,'" read Lexie, peering at the notices. "'Broadway Bound'—that's a trip to see a musical. 'The Spring Flower Show. A Tasting Tour of Manhattan'—that's something to do with restaurants. Wow, Daddy Bo, you're going to be busy."

"I never!" he said, and I wasn't positive what he meant, but his eyes were kind of sparkling, so that was good.

We peeked in the library, which was bigger than my school library, and then we peeked in the lecture room, and after that we took the elevator to the second floor. I examined the crafts room and looked hopefully for a sign announcing grandfather/granddaughter art classes, but I didn't see one. I did see, though, that Daddy Bo was smiling again, and this was nice since his smile had been missing for quite some time.

Finally Lexie looked at her watch and said, "We'd better go back upstairs. It's one o'clock. Mom and Dad will be wondering where we are."

On the fifth floor we found Daddy Bo's apartment and when we opened the door we saw that Mom and Dad had unpacked every box we'd brought. The place looked pretty much like Daddy Bo's house in New Jersey, except with a view of Seventy-second Street out the window.

We ate lunch in the coffee shop, and later we went back to the fifth floor. We rode in the elevator with a man wearing a baseball cap and holding a cane, who was very cheerful, and when he got off with us and saw where we were going, he said to Daddy Bo, "You must be our new neighbor. I'm Howard. I live across the hall in 5D. Why don't you join my wife and me for dinner tonight?"

I was only a little jealous that Howard and his wife would get to have dinner with Daddy Bo, and anyway, I decided that this was one of those things that shouldn't get out in the open, so I didn't mention it.

"Well," said my father, looking around Daddy Bo's new place, "I think you're pretty well set here, Dad."

That was my father's way of saying it was time for us to leave.

"We'll be back tomorrow," added my mother. "We're all going to go out for brunch."

"I remember," said Daddy Bo.

We started to put on our coats.

"Daddy Bo," I said, "I have something for you." I reached into my pocket and handed my grandfather an envelope with his name on it and a box that I had wrapped in tinfoil and tied with a piece of yarn.

"Goodness, what's this, Pearl?" he said.

He opened the envelope first and found the card I'd made for him. On the outside it said To the best grand-farther in the world and showed a picture of Daddy Bo standing on a globe with the squirrel tail attached to his pants. On the inside it said I WILL MISS YOU!!! and showed a picture of me crying.

"Thank you very much," said Daddy Bo.

"Now open the box," I told him.

Daddy Bo did so and he found a key on a key chain.

"I made the key chain," I announced.

"It's beautiful, Pearl. But what's the key to?"

"To me," I replied.

23

Back at our apartment, my old room was empty. Or almost empty. My bed was still there, of course, and my dresser and my desk. But Daddy Bo's things were gone from the closet, and on top of the dresser was nothing and on top of the desk was nothing. Daddy Bo had kept pictures on the desk—my school picture and Lexie's school picture and a picture of my dead grandmother (before she died) and a picture of my father when he was little and a picture of some dog I didn't know. And he had put all sorts of things on the dresser—mail and handkerchiefs and a seashell I had painted for him and paper clips and magazines and packages of gum. But these things had been packed up and moved to The Towers and now my room looked like it had never belonged to anyone at all.

Lexie came out of her room and stood in my doorway. "So," she said, "I guess you can have your room back."

I think what she wanted to say was, "I guess *I* can have *my* room back," but she was a little politer these days. She even let me spend one more night in her room. The next morning, though, before we even left to take Daddy Bo out to brunch, we began to lug loads of my stuff down the hall to my room, and by that night we were finished. The last thing Lexie did was take down the LEXIE AND PEARL'S ROOM sign. But she didn't throw it away. "I'll just keep it in my desk for a while," she said. I knew she was only being polite, but whatever.

One afternoon, a couple of weeks after Daddy Bo had left, I passed by Lexie's room and since the door was open I leaned inside and said, "You know what?"

Lexie was plugging away at her homework. "What?"

"The days used to seem really long, but now they go by quickly."

"That's because you're busier."

"Really?"

"Definitely. It's a fact." Lexie closed her textbook and gave me her full attention. "When you're busier, time passes faster. I mean, it *seems* to pass faster. Like, when you're sick? And you spend the day in bed? You know how long the day feels? But when you're busy with school and homework and friends and projects, the days fly by."

"I guess." Personally, I thought Lexie sounded like a magazine article, but then I considered what she'd said and decided maybe it was true. Back in the fall I had slogged through school and then in the afternoons Justine usually came over but she never knew what she wanted to do so I had to play Sorry! for both of us, etc., etc., etc. But these days things were different. In school I hung out with James Brubaker the Third. We passed notes in class and we ate together in the cafeteria and we played Spy during roof time. At first we spied on Rachel and Katie and Jill, but it turned out that they weren't all that interesting, so then we spied on imaginary enemies like giant sewer rats and men carrying suspicious briefcases. We kept a notebook labeled SPY NOTATIONS and hoped Rachel or Katie or Jill would steal it, since we had also written fake stuff about them in it, but they were too concerned with their fingernails and hair.

After school JBIII would come over to my apartment or I would go over to his and it was nice to play games with someone who could read the directions. At exactly 4:30 every afternoon, though, JBIII would say that it was time for him to do his homework, and then he would go home, or else I would have to leave his apartment and go home myself. (JBIII's name had never once been written in the corner of the blackboard in Mr. Potter's room and he said he planned to keep it that way.)

Then when I was alone in my room I would work hard on our assignments about myths and crustaceans and verbs. And sometimes JBIII would call me at night and say, "Don't forget your math worksheets," or whatever, so then I would put them in my backpack, and all in all everyone was pretty pleased with me.

Mr. Potter sent home progress reports and my parents were so happy with mine that they phoned Daddy Bo and said, "Guess what. Pearl got her best report ever! She improved in every single subject." Daddy Bo asked to speak to me then, and he said, "Blimey, Pirate Pearl! You've done a bang-up job!" which I don't think "bang-up" is a pirate term, but whatever.

Anyway, what with JBIII and my homework and visiting Daddy Bo on the weekends, the time was flying by, so Lexie's theory was probably correct.

I thought Lexie might pick up her textbook again, but instead she said, "Hey, Pearl, who do you think is going to move into Justine's apartment?"

I was quiet for a moment, remembering my old best friend. Then I thought about the news John had given Lexie and me after school that day—that somebody had bought the Lebarros' apartment. But John didn't know anything about the new owners.

"I don't know," I replied. "I hope they have a kid exactly my age, though. Oh! Maybe they'll be foreign and I'll have to teach them English."

Lexie turned her face away from me for a moment, but then she said, "So who's coming to your birthday party?"

There was a lot of news about my party. For starters, when I had told my parents that Justine would be in Paris on my birthday, Dad had said, "Why don't you have your party early this year, Pearl? If you have it before school lets out, no one will be on vacation yet."

So I planned my party for a Saturday in May. At first my guest list only included Justine and JBIII. But JBIII convinced me to invite five kids from our grade too. And then guess what. It turned out that Justine wouldn't be home *then* either, but the invitations—which I had made myself—had already been sent out, so I couldn't change the date.

"Leslie's coming," I said to Lexie, "and Elena and Kenny and Greg and Elyse. I don't think you know them. But they're nice."

I left my sister alone then, since I had learned a thing or two about overstaying my welcome, and I went to my room to think about my birthday list. I knew my family would give me their presents on my actual birthday in the summer, but I didn't think it could hurt to get a head start on the list. (The list wasn't going to come as a surprise to anyone anyway, since all I wanted was the cell phone, the computer, and the key to our apartment.)

One day Lexie dropped me off at our building after school and when the elevator doors opened on the seventh floor I heard voices and loud noises. The door to Justine's apartment was open and I could see boxes and furniture in the front hall. I tiptoed to the doorway and peeked inside. In my head I was saying, "Please let my new neighbor be a nine-year-old girl. And please let her have her own cell phone and computer and key to the apartment." If she had any of those things, I would be sure to mention the fact to my parents.

"Hello? Can I help you?"

I jumped.

A young woman had stepped out of the living room. She was carrying a baby.

"I'm sorry," I said. "I wasn't spying or anything." Even though I was. "My name is Pearl. I live in Seven-F."

The woman smiled. "I'm Nancy Harmer. And this"— she waved the baby's fist at me—"is Matthew."

"Do you have any other kids?" I asked hopefully.

"Nope. It's just Matty and my husband and me."

Oh. Undoubtedly, Lexie would get to be Matty's babysitter and earn lots of money. But I remembered my manners and tried to look like I was thrilled to have a baby down the hall.

I waved good-bye to Mrs. Harmer.

That afternoon I made some notes about my birthday party. I had decided that my guests could spend the afternoon making crafts. We were going to have different stations set up in the family room: one for painting T-shirts, one for making beaded bracelets, one for decorating treasure boxes, and one for sand art. I had also decided what we were going to eat at the party: bagels with different toppings, and for dessert fruit kabobs.

My mother had said, "Pearl, don't you want to have your party at the bowling alley?"

My father had said, "Or at the gymnastics center?"

And my sister had said, "The guests will want pizza and cake and ice cream, not bagels and fruit kabobs."

But it was my party and I knew what I wanted.

24

The very first person to arrive at my birthday party was Daddy Bo. My father had taken the subway to The Towers in the morning and picked up Daddy Bo, who now stood in our living room looking around at the craft stations.

"Gracious, Pearl. This is a wonder!" His chin flap swayed slightly.

"Thank you," I said modestly. "See, at this table everybody gets to paint a T-shirt. And over here they can make bracelets. If the boys don't want bracelets for themselves, they can make them for their mothers or something. Over *here* is the table for sand art sculptures. And at the big table is all the stuff you need to decorate a treasure box. You can use paint or glitter or sequins or even feathers. Or everything all at once for a very fancy box."

I took Daddy Bo's hand, led him into t
showed him the party food. "First we're
our own bagels," I said. "Look at all the
nut butter and cream cheese and jam and
I don't know why anyone would want it
if you don't know what lox is, it's thin slices or this
slimy pink fish that's as limp as a wet washcloth and
smells like the inside of your shoes. But some people
like it.

"And for dessert, make-your-own fruit kabobs." I
showed Daddy Bo the dishes of strawberries and pieces
of melon and apple and pineapple and pear, waiting
to be stabbed onto fancy skewers shaped like pirate
swords.

"What a creative birthday party, Pearl," said Daddy Bo.

"Lexie and Valerie and Lindsey are going to help out,"
I told him, "and they're not even getting paid. They just
wanted to come."

The doorbell rang then and I answered it to find
James Brubaker the Third standing in the hall holding a
present that was pretty much shaped like a book.

"Happy birthday!" he said.

"Thank you. Come on in. Look at all the stations."

JBIII had helped me plan everything for the party, but
he hadn't seen the stations in the family room yet, except if he had tried to spy from across the street.

I set his present on the floor by the couch. The

rang again and this time Valerie and Lindsey arrived. Perfect. I wanted to make sure they knew how to help out with the crafts. Lexie too. I was introducing them to the stations when Bitey jumped up on the treasure box table and landed in a pile of pink and blue feathers.

"Perhaps Bitey should spend the party in your room, Pearl," said my mother, and she carried him away, feathers drifting off his back as they passed by.

Daddy Bo sat down on the couch then and said, "Now, what time is the party due to start, Pearl?" and suddenly I remembered Thanksgiving with the Lebarros. But before I could get too worried, the doorbell rang for a third time, and then a fourth and a fifth, and soon all the rest of my guests had arrived. Mom brought Daddy Bo a cup of coffee and he sat on the couch with a smile on his face.

At first my guests seemed a little uncertain. Leslie stood in the doorway of the family room, biting her thumbnail and gripping Elyse's arm. Kenny and Greg huddled together in front of the windows, laughing about something private. And Elena sat by herself at the opposite end of the couch from Daddy Bo, looking like she might cry.

But then JBIII announced, "Okay, everybody. Time for the crafts. Kenny and Greg, why don't you decorate T-shirts? I'm going to make a bracelet."

Kenny and Greg looked shocked as they watched JBIII sit on the floor with a needle and a tin of red beads and get to work. But then I began to paint a pirate skull on a T-shirt, and before I knew it, Kenny and Greg were copying my design. When I looked around the room a little while later I saw Leslie and Elyse gluing sequins to wooden boxes. And at the sand art station sat Elena and Daddy Bo, each making a sculpture.

"What a treat!" I heard Daddy Bo say, and Elena smiled at him.

It took a long time for everyone to make every item, and when Mom said, "Who wants to take a break for bagels?" no one raised their hand. Kenny was only half-way done with a yellow and green bracelet, I was in the middle of writing TREASURES on a box, Greg was taking his turn at sand art, JBIII was sketching a portrait of Bitey (from memory) on a T-shirt, and the girls were having their faces decorated by Valerie, who had brought face paints as a surprise.

Later, though, when everyone had made one bracelet and one T-shirt and one sculpture and one box, I stood in the middle of the family room and said, "And now it is time for make-your-own bagels!"

Lexie and Valerie and Lindsey had cleared the family room table and spread out the bagels and the toppings. My guests each took a plate and set to work. JBIII was the only one who put lox on his bagel. He said lox tasted just like the ocean and made him think of the beach. I watched as Elena spread peanut butter on her bagel and made a face with jam. Greg dropped a little of every single topping except the lox onto his bagel. Kenny scooped a huge mound of tunafish onto his bagel and called it the Eiffel Tower.

No one said anything about wanting pizza.

After the bagels came the fruit kabobs. I think my guests liked the pirate swords more than the fruit, but whatever. By then Elena was laughing, and Leslie and Elyse had stopped clinging to each other, and Kenny and Greg had asked Valerie if she would paint their faces.

JBIII suddenly got a funny look, like he'd had some sort of idea, and he left the family room. He returned carrying Bitey. "Presenting the pirate king!" cried JBIII. He set Bitey on the couch, which he called a pirate ship, and tried to get him to pose with a fruit kabob sword, but Bitey took a flying leap off the couch and escaped from the room by way of the food table. He knocked the lox and the rest of the pineapple onto the floor, and Dad said, "Ahem," and JBIII said, "Sorry," and then all the parents started to arrive anyway.

The party was over.

"That was the most fun I've had in a long time," announced Daddy Bo as the door closed behind JBIII, who was the last to leave.

"Me too." I looked at the stack of presents my friends had given me. I would open them later, after we had cleaned up the family room.

I helped Mom and Dad get everything back in order and then Daddy Bo and I took a little nap before dinner. We sat on the couch with *The Wizard of Oz* playing on TV and pretended we were awake, but really we were not.

Later, when our nap was over, I gazed fondly at the tower of presents. I wanted to open them right away, but Mom and Dad wanted us to have dinner first. I waited about six more minutes and then I wailed, "*Please* don't make me wait any longer!"

So everyone gathered in the family room, I settled on the floor with the gifts from my friends, and Mom sat at the table with a pen and a pad of paper so she could keep a list of the thank-you notes I would have to write. I tried not to look at her. There is nothing like watching someone keep a list of work you'll have to do while you're trying to enjoy opening presents.

All of my friends had brought me art supplies, except for JBIII, who had gotten me a book about pirates. It came with a pirate map and included songs about pirates and information on pirate clothing. I was taking a good look at the costumes when suddenly my mother stood up and said, "Oh! I almost forgot." And she left the family room and hurried into her office. When she came back she was holding a small wrapped package. "This is from Dad and me," she said. "An early birthday present."

The box wasn't big enough to be either a computer or a cell phone, but that was okay. I untied the ribbon and lifted the lid.

Inside the box was a key.

"Is it to our apartment?" I asked, hoping Mom wouldn't say, "No, it's the key to me," which would have been horribly disappointing.

Mom nodded.

"Really?" I jumped up, ran to the front door, opened it, and tested the key. It worked.

"Here's a key chain," added my father.

I hugged my mother and my father and Daddy Bo and Lexie. Then I hung my very own key and key chain in the kitchen next to everyone else's personal keys.

Before I went to bed that night I sat at my desk, pulled out the comparison chart, and studied it. On the "Interests" line I added "art" underneath "stuffed animals." Then I got out an eraser. On the "Has Own Key to Apartment" line I erased the "no" in the Pearl column and replaced it with a "yes." I thought about how on Monday when I went to the lobby to pick up our mail, I could use my new key. I would be sure to show it to John. And of course to JBIII.

I slid the chart into my desk drawer, called good night to Lexie and my parents, and crawled into bed. A moment later I felt a thump as Bitey landed on my chest. "Night, Bitey," I said, and he began to purr loudly.

	☺ LeXie	☺ PeaYl
Age	13 going on 14	9 (just barely)
Full Name	Alexandria	Pearl
Interests	violin ballay gymnastics soccer knitting school baby sitting	stuffed animals art
Room	neat	sloppy
Friends ♡	Valerie (best friend) Sophia, Polly Chloe, Emma B. Emma F.	Justine (neighbor/ first-grader) James Brubaker the Third (boy)
Boyfriend	Dallas	Bitey (cat) 🐱
Lipstick	yes	no
Awards	yes	no
Chews Gum	no	yes

Pest	no	yes
Wears a Bra	yes	no
Has Had Apendix Out	no	yes
Has Thrown Up in a Taxicab	no	yes 😵
Has Own Key to Apartment	⌐━◎ yes	⌐━◎ yes
Stuck up	yes	no
Has Thrown up in Own Bed	yes	no
Cavities	4	0

GO FISH

ANN M. MARTIN

What sparked your imagination for _Ten Rules for Living with My Sister_?
Pearl's voice and character came to me before her story did. I liked the idea of this girl who's very outspoken, yet still not quite sure of her place in the world. And I wanted to explore Pearl's relationship with her older sister—a sister Pearl idolizes, yet manages to drive crazy.

When you were a child, did you ever experience friends moving away?
None of my close friends moved away when I was growing up, but my sister's best friend moved clear across the country. I didn't want to do that to Pearl. I wanted Pearl and Justine to be able to see each other from time to time. Still, Justine's move was very difficult for Pearl. At the same time, it allowed her to branch out and find another friend.

Did you grow up with any sisters?
I have one sister, Jane. She's two years younger than me. We fought and we also had a lot of fun together, but we had a different relationship than Pearl and Lexie do in the book since Jane and I are much closer in age.

Did you have any rules for living with each other?
No, we didn't have any rules. Maybe we should have. I will say that while we were very different from each other when we were younger, now we're best friends.

What is your favorite Halloween costume to dress up as?
I don't have a favorite, but when I was a kid, the one I was the most proud of was the leprechaun costume that I sewed for myself when I was eleven!

Where do you write your books?
I can write anywhere as long as it's quiet. At the moment, I'm writing at the dining-room table.

Where do you find inspiration for your writing?
I never know where it's going to come from. Sometimes I remember an incident from my childhood, sometimes I hear about something on the news that interests me, sometimes a character presents herself and a story grows up around the character.

When you finish a book, who reads it first?
My editor. I don't usually share my work with anyone else. My editor reads each book in stages while I'm writing it.

What do you like best about being an author?
My favorite thing about being an author is being able to create characters and tell their stories. There's something exciting and freeing about the storytelling process. There are lots of ways to tell stories—in pictures, in words, in movies. I love getting caught up in the lives of my characters. Sometimes I tell my characters' stories and sometimes the characters tell their stories themselves.

What did you want to be when you grew up?
Although I always enjoyed writing, I wanted to be a teacher when I grew up. In fact, I majored in elementary education, got my teaching degree, and taught in a small private school after I graduated from college. But by that time, writing and children's literature were becoming important to me, so I entered the publishing field and worked as an editor while I wrote my first few books.

When did you realize you wanted to be a writer?
It was after I had entered the publishing field and was working on children's books that I decided to write seriously. I started my first novel when I was twenty-five.

What's your first childhood memory?
I remember my grandfather pushing me on a swing in our backyard and singing "My Bonnie Lies over the Ocean" to me. I was about three years old.

As a young person, who did you look up to most?
My father. We were very close. He's a cartoonist, and he encouraged my interest in writing and in art. I thought everything he did was wonderful. He's very fanciful and imaginative, and took my sister and me to carnivals and magic shows, and made up stories about a little man named Mr. Piebald who lived in the woods behind our house.

What was your worst subject in school?
Math.

What was your best subject in school?
Language arts, French, creative writing—anything to do with words.

What was your first job?
When I was a kid—babysitting; as an adult—working with children with autism.

Are you a morning person or a night owl?
Definitely a morning person. I'm usually wide awake by 5 AM—and falling asleep by 10 PM. When I was little, my parents used to bribe me to stay in bed until seven in the morning so I wouldn't wake them up so early.

What's your idea of the best meal ever?
Salmon, brussels sprout, olives, a large salad, and for dessert, plenty of chocolate or maybe my sister's ginger pudding.

Which do you like better: cats or dogs?
I can't choose one over the other. I like them both. I have one dog and three cats.

What do you value most in your friends?
A sense of humor and the ability to keep a secret.

Where do you go for peace and quiet?
To my sewing room.

What makes you laugh out loud?
I Love Lucy.

What's your favorite song?
"Dream a Little Dream of Me," but my favorite composer is Gershwin, and my favorite Gershwin piece is "Rhapsody in Blue."

Who is your favorite fictional character?
Scout Finch from *To Kill a Mockingbird*.

What are you most afraid of?
Snakes and spiders.

What time of year do you like best?
Summer. Winter is my second favorite season.

If you were stranded on a desert island, who would you want for company?
Anyone who could figure out how to get us off the island. I would also like to be with my dog. She's very good company.

If you could travel in time, where would you go?
I'd like to travel about fifty years into the future, just to see what's going on. Then I'd like to go back to New York City at the beginning of the twentieth century.

What would you do if you ever stopped writing?
I would like to concentrate on sewing and needlework, take some knitting classes and a beading class, learn to speak Italian, and see Hawaii and the Grand Canyon.

What do you like best about yourself?
I'm never, ever bored.

What is your worst habit?
I'm easily distracted.

Where in the world do you feel most at home?
In my sewing room. It's my favorite place.

What do you wish you could do better?
I wish I weren't so shy and that I were better at public speaking.

What would your readers be most surprised to learn about you?
I also wish I were better at tap dancing.

Pearl must write an essay about her summer, but that's not an easy task. Her dad lost his job, Pearl had to attend a camp where her sister was a counselor-in-training, and a fight with James Brubaker the Third landed one of them in the hospital!

Experience Pearl's summer adventures in

1

"Lexie?" I said on the first day of fifth grade. "Are you nervous about school?"

It was 6:10 a.m., and I was in the hall outside my big sister's bedroom, leaning backward against her door, talking largely to the air. Lexie used to hang a NO PEARL sign on the door to keep me out, but these days I was welcome in her room as long as I was (a) fully clothed, since Lexie still didn't approve of underwear visits, and (b) prepared to start a meaningful conversation. Like, I couldn't interrupt her homework or her violin practice to say, "If Bitey died and then came back to life as a human, do you think he would ask me to marry him?" (Bitey is our cat.) Or, "Have you kissed your new boy-friend yet?" Actually, I thought the kissing question could start a very meaningful conversation, but Lexie never seemed to want to discuss either her boyfriend or kissing with me.

There was no answer from within Lexie's room. In fact, there was no sound at all in our apartment. That was probably because it was 6:10 a.m. Everyone was still asleep. Everyone except me, Pearl Littlefield. I was nervous about starting fifth grade. And I was curious to find out whether Lexie was nervous about starting high school.

"Lexie?" I said again. "Lexie?"

I heard a thump from my parents' room and decided to lower my voice.

"Lexie?" I said in a loud whisper.

"Pearl, WHAT?" replied my sister suddenly, yanking her door open. I fell into her room and landed on my bottom. "What are you doing? It isn't even six fifteen yet."

I got to my feet. "Are you nervous about school?"

Lexie clapped her hand to her forehead and flung herself on her bed. "You're asking me this now?"

Well, duh. It was the first day of school. When was I supposed to ask? "I need to know," I told her.

Lexie rolled her eyes. Or at least I think she did. She'd already closed her lids, but I could see that her eyeballs were rolling around underneath. "I guess so," she replied finally. "Everyone is nervous on the first day of school, Pearl."

"No, not everyone. I don't think JBThree is nervous."

JBIII is my new best friend. His complete name is James Brubaker the Third, but I shortened it to JBIII, which when you say it out loud it's JBThree.

"So maybe you should talk to JBThree," said Lexie, "and let me go back to sleep."

Her alarm rang then and she made a face at me, but frankly, it wasn't as mean a face as she would have made a few months ago. She turned off the alarm, patted me on the shoulder as she headed for the bathroom, and said, "You'll be fine, Pearl."

An hour and a half later I called good-bye to Mom and rode to the lobby of our apartment building with my father and Lexie and Lexie's cell phone. There's no cell-phone reception on elevators, but my sister had gotten a head start on her phone call by already speed-dialing her best friend Valerie's number. Now her thumb was poised over the Send button, prepared to press it the very second she stepped out of the elevator, so as not to waste a moment contacting Valerie about important high school business. But she didn't have to do that. When the elevator doors opened there were Valerie and also the two Emmas sitting on the couch in the lobby across from John, my favorite doorman. They were wearing a lot of black eyeliner and staring at their cell phones and not talking. But when they saw Lexie they jumped up, and the four of them started squealing and hugging like they hadn't just been together the afternoon before.

"Bye, Dad! Bye, Pearl!" called Lexie, and she and her grown-up high school friends rushed out the door and onto Twelfth Street.

When you're fourteen you don't need an adult to take you to school, even if you live in New York City. When you're ten you do. Also, just so you know, when you're fourteen you get to have a cell phone and your own personal computer. When you're ten, you don't. (Well, I don't.)

Dad and I walked past John, who gave me a high five and said, "Break a leg, Pearl," which is a nice thing to say, not a mean one, except you're supposed to say it to actors not students, but whatever.

We stepped outside and I looked across Twelfth Street, and there was JBIII coming out of his building with his mother who wanted to take a first-day-of-school picture. JBIII posed for one half of one second, and then joined Dad and me for the walk to Emily Dickinson Elementary.

"Remember the first day of school last year?" I said to my father. "You walked Justine and me to Emily Dickinson. This year you're walking JBThree and me."

"Things certainly do change," replied Dad, and I thought he looked a little sad. That was because there had been a lot of changes in our lives besides who I walked to school with.

We turned the corner onto Sixth Avenue and passed by all the familiar places in our neighborhood: New World, which is a coffee shop, and Steve-Dan's, which is my all-time favorite store because it sells art supplies, and Cuppa Joe, which is a new coffee shop, and Universal, which is a dry cleaner, and the Daily Grind, which is *another* new coffee shop. Over the summer Lexie and her friends started going to the Daily Grind to order Mocha Moxies, which they say are coffee drinks but which really look like giant milk shakes. Whenever Lexie starts talking about how she's grown-up enough to drink coffee what I want to say back to her is, "Mom and Dad don't squirt a tower of whipped cream on top of their coffee," but one thing I have learned lately is when not to say something.

When Dad and JBIII and I passed Monk's, which is a gift store, I could feel JBIII's eyes on me. Well, not actually *on* me, which would be gross, but suddenly I could tell he was looking at me and I knew why. We were now one half of a block away from Emily Dickinson, and JBIII and I had decided that no matter what anyone thought, we were simply too old to be walked right up to the door of our school by a parent.

"Dad," I said, "JBThree and I are ten years old now." (JBIII was actually a lot closer to eleven, while I was just barely ten.)

"Yes, you are," agreed Dad.

"And we think that—" JBIII frowned fiercely at me and I tried to remember the exact speech he had made me memorize the day before. "I mean," I said, backing up, "and we feel strongly that we should be allowed"—JBIII poked my arm—"that, um, we're responsible enough to walk the rest of the way to school by ourselves. Every day."

"You can stand here and watch us," said JBIII. And then he added quickly, "Sir."

"Well . . . ," said my father.

Dad has let me do this 2x before, but now JBIII and I were asking to do it regularly, and my father has a teensy problem with change, whether it's good or bad.

"*Please?*" I said, and now JBIII glared at me. He had also warned me not to whine. "Please, Father?" I said calmly.

"I suppose so."

"Yes!" I exclaimed.

"Thank you, sir," said JBIII.

"But remember—I'll be watching you."

"I know," I said. "Don't kiss me," I added, and JBIII and I ran down the block. Just before we reached Emily Dickinson I waved backward over my shoulder to Dad.

JBIII and I wound our way through the halls of Emily Dickinson. We passed by the first-grade room that Justine

Lebarro had been in the year before, and then we passed our old fourth-grade room. There was Mr. Potter, our teacher from last year, talking to his new students.

We kept on walking until we came to room 5A. I peeked through the doorway, then stepped back and flattened myself against the wall like a spy. "She's in there," I whispered to JBIII. "Ms. Brody."

Our teacher was new to Emily Dickinson. All we knew about her was her name.

JBIII peeked in, too. "She looks all right," he whispered to me.

The truth was that she looked very, very young, like if you switched her pants and her shirt for a white dress and a veil she could be a bride. I kept that thought to myself, though, because I could just hear Lexie clucking her tongue and saying to me, "A person can get married at any age, Pearl." But still in my head all brides were young.

"Afraid to go in?" said a voice from behind JBIII and me, and we both jumped.

I turned around to see Jill DiNunzio, who is a person I could live without.

"No," I said, doing an eye roll.

"So what are you waiting for?" she asked.

"Well, not you. Come on, JBThree."

JBIII and I marched into our new classroom, leaving Jill behind.

Fifth grade had officially begun.

Ms. Brody let us sit wherever we wanted, at least to begin with. So JBIII and I chose seats together in the last row. I had always wanted to have a best friend to sit with on the first day of school. And it was a relief not to wind up sitting directly in front of the teacher's desk like I did in Mr. Potter's room so he could keep an eye on me.

I watched Jill look around and take a seat by the window. I expected her to save seats for Rachel and Katie, but before I knew what had happened, Ms. Brody had closed the door to our room and said, "Welcome, fifth graders."

I raised my eyebrows. All the seats were taken.

Jill-Rachel-Katie had been split up. I almost jumped out of my chair and cried, "Yes!" but adults don't usually like that sort of thing and I wanted to make a good impression on Ms. Brody so she wouldn't be too mad the first time I left my homework papers under my bed or ran out of steam on a vocab assignment. (I am not a big fan of vocab.)

Ms. Brody began to talk about the things we would be studying in fifth grade, so I turned my attention to Jill and how she probably wouldn't be able to wield any power in our classroom all by herself. By the look of things, she didn't have any close friends at all in room 5A. And I had JBIII.

I could tell it was going to be a good year.

Next I thought about Lexie being in high school. I wondered what she and Valerie and the Emmas were doing right at that exact second. Then I thought about Bitey for a while, and then my parents, and finally I heard the word "homework."

Homework? Really? On the very first day of school? This seemed unfair.

"I want you to write an essay about your summer vacation," Ms. Brody was saying. "Please outline what you're going to write about, and then write from the outline."

Hmm. I thought that over. How would Ms. Brody know whether we had written an outline? I could probably skip that step.

"And please hand in both the outline and your essay tomorrow," Ms. Brody finished up.

I glanced at JBIII, all prepared to make a face about the awfulness of fifth grade, but he was taking notes on practically every word Ms. Brody said, since one thing he always does is every single assignment.

When school finally ended and JBIII and I were walking home ten steps ahead of my father (I didn't want to be rude, but really, it wasn't as if I hadn't walked the route to and from Emily Dickinson about 900x in my life), JBIII said to me, "Our essays are going to be pretty long, Pearl."

"I guess." I didn't want to think about homework just then.

"Let's go to your apartment and start them right now. We have a lot to write about."

I wanted JBIII to come over, but I did not want to start my homework. "Let's draw," I said to him, thinking longingly of my art supplies.

"Nope," said JBIII, but not in a mean way. "I want to do a good job on our first assignment for Ms. Brody."

"All right," I said at last.

As soon as we'd eaten a snack of apples and cheese sticks, JBIII and I sat down side by side on the floor of my bedroom. In the old days we would have settled in the family room, which is really the family room, living room, and dining room all in the same space. But recently the family room had become my father's office and he was sitting there now, glaring at his computer screen.

"Now," said JBIII in a businesslike voice, a pad of paper propped against his knees, "first things first." In his neatest printing he wrote MY SUMMER VACATION—OUTLINE across the top of the first sheet of paper. He moved his pencil to the line below. "One," he said aloud, and wrote a Roman numeral one.

Oh, yeah. You're supposed to use Roman numerals on an outline. An interesting thing about Roman numerals is that JBIII has one in his name. III=3 in regular numbers.

I watched JBIII scratch busily away, making notes

about his summer, and I tried to remember how Roman numerals go. Then I thought for a while about Rome, which made me remember an exhibit on Rome that had been at the Museum of Natural History on one of the worst days of my life. It was the end of third grade and our class had taken a field trip to the museum and suddenly I couldn't find my classmates, only dinosaur skeletons, so I shouted, "Help! Police!" and got quite a few adults, including Mrs. DiNunzio (Jill's mother) and our teacher, in trouble for losing me. After that, the other third graders would whisper "Help! Police!" in my ear whenever they wanted to annoy me, which was pretty often, since they already thought I was a big baby. The incident at the museum might not have been so bad if there hadn't been two other incidents that year, one involving Show and Tell (which how was I supposed to know you don't have Show and Tell anymore when you get to third grade in Emily Dickinson Elementary?) and one involving my tinkle. Yes, there was an accidental wetting of my pants, but I don't want to go into the embarrassing details here. All you really need to know is that the whole year was embarrassing and that Jill and Rachel and Katie thought that every bad thing that happened to me was hilarious. Then we all turned up together in the same fourth-grade class, but by the end of that year JBIII and I had become friends, so I didn't care so much about Jill-Rachel-Katie.

"Pearl?" said JBIII.

"Yeah?"

"Aren't you going to start your outline?"

I looked at JBIII's paper, which was all spotted with Roman numerals and notes to himself. Then I looked at mine, which was blank.

"I'm still collecting my thoughts," I told him, and luckily at that moment, JBIII's mother phoned because she wanted him to come home.

When he left, I sat down at the desk, and opened my notebook. After a very long time I wrote MY SUMMER VACATION—OUTLINE across the top, and then I made a capital letter I on the next line, which is how you write a Roman numeral one.

I stared and stared at the I, and at last I turned to a clean page in my notebook. What would be much, much more fun than writing an outline would be making questionnaires for my parents to fill out at dinnertime. I wrote Mom's in pink ink and Dad's in green.

Name _____

Age _____

Address _____

_____

Telephone numbers:

    Home _____

    Cell _____

Interests_____

_____

_____

Home: good _____ bad _____

Has husband or husband and children:

    yes _____ no _____

Likes cats: yes _____ no _____

Loves her family dearly: yes _____ no _____

This was Mom's questionnaire. I made a similar one for my father.

Then I settled down to start my outline. Next to the Roman numeral I I wrote: My dad got fired.